Remember when a good love story made you feel like holding hands?

Harlequin presents

LEOPARD
in the
SNOW
...*a love story*

Coming soon to a theater near you!

OTHER
Harlequin Romances
by REBECCA STRATTON

Spindrift

by

REBECCA STRATTON

Harlequin Books

TORONTO • LONDON • NEW YORK • AMSTERDAM • SYDNEY

Original hardcover edition published in 1977
by Mills & Boon Limited

ISBN 0-373-02173-9

Harlequin edition published June 1978

PRINTED IN U.S.A.

CHAPTER ONE

OUT at sea a trading schooner ploughed its way through the deep blue Caribbean, the white foaming wash of its progress dancing around it and giving the impression that it floated on a reflection of the blue sky with its spindrift of white cloud. It was a seemingly lazy progress, but in fact the trade winds made for excellent going, and the effect on the eye was stunning.

The small trader was fully rigged and most likely making for Guadeloupe and the port of Basse-terre, and with its sails billowing in the brisk wind and seen against the ever-changing background of sea and sky it was a sight that had changed little in a hundred years.

It was a sight that had become familiar to Bryony Charn during the past eight years, and one which never failed to attract her, although her attention was rather more casual today than it usually was. She sat with Tim, her half-brother, beside her, hugging her knees and watching the trader with absent eyes, only vaguely aware of the matchless beauty of it.

In the shadow of the coconut palms her face was thoughtful. The same palms grew in a green fringe all around the island's beaches, bowed into sweeping curves, so that their rough hairy trunks almost touched the sand in places, where the winds had blown them low in to obeisance. White sand that glittered diamond bright in the hot Caribbean sun.

In such a setting life could be idyllic, but at the moment Tim was unhappy, and when Tim was unhappy it was inevitable that Bryony was too. Although he was two years older than she was, the two of them were so near in age and so much younger than most of the family that a rapport had grown up between them that is more often found between twins.

Tim was a Charn, just as she was herself, but the island was Laminaire property, and they were constantly kept aware of it. The original Laminaire to inhabit Petitnue was reputed to have been the product of an Algerian pirate and one of his pretty French captives and, looking at Dominic, the latest of the line, Bryony could quite easily believe it was true.

There was a dark, rakish arrogance about him that stirred the imagination and encouraged it to indulge in fantasies about swashbuckling, dusky-skinned buccaneers who took what they wanted and gave no quarter. To Bryony, Dominic Laminaire was the most discomfiting feature of Petitnue as well as its owner, and yet she could not imagine the island without him.

Bryony had never really known what stroke of chance originally brought Rupert Charn, the young Englishman who was to be both her and Tim's father, to this tiny and beautiful island in the Caribbean, but his arrival had changed his life and made it possible for Bryony to be there now.

Only a month after his arrival he had married the young widow Laminaire and become at once both husband and father, for his new wife already had a three-year-old son. In less than a year he had a son of his own, and ten years later still another son was born, one who cost Louise Charn her life. It was Timothy, this younger son, who now sat with Bryony, pondering on his future so gloomily.

Bryony herself was the only child of an ill-fated second marriage, also contracted in haste but much less successful. The young Englishwoman he married while she was on holiday in the West Indies had become homesick and returned to England and never came back, so that Bryony was ten years old before she saw her father.

It was soon after her mother died that a tall, tanned stranger came and whisked her away to this strange and exotic world where she found herself suddenly part of a family that included her father and two half-brothers as well as a grown-up stepbrother. A man whom she could never somehow consider as in any way related to her, even by marriage.

By the time Bryony arrived tension was already growing between her father and Dominic, his stepson. Dominic was a Laminaire and considered himself the natural successor to his father. Rupert Charn, who had run the plantation since his first marriage, saw no reason to relinquish the reins to his stepson, but at twenty-six Dominic thought it high time he came into his own, and there was constant friction between them by the time Bryony came.

The situation had resolved itself a little less than two years later when Rupert Charn died, and Bryony had passed, apparently quite automatically, to the guardianship of his stepson, Dominic Laminaire. Petitnue was back in the hands of the Laminaires, as it had been for centuries.

Dominic was twenty-eight by then and much too busy to take on the tutoring of a twelve-year-old girl, as her father had done, so there had been little she could do about his sending her to school on the British island of Dominica—a little English school where she had learned what utter loneliness meant for the first time. She still remembered how she had wept each time she was returned there after her monthly week-end visits.

By the time she was seventeen, just over a year ago now, she had made up her mind that she would not go back to school, and she had taken the bull by the horns and informed Dominic of the fact. Surprisingly he had not opposed the idea, but agreed that she had all the schooling she needed, even though it had done little to subdue a fairly rebellious nature. Since then she had lived at home and managed to make herself both useful and happy; the latter because of her close relationships with both Tim and her sister-in-law.

Jules, the elder of her half-brothers, was married, and it had made a great deal of difference having Jenny living on the island. Another woman in the family had given her a confidante, and she always took her griev-ances to Jenny, a fact that Jules often teased her about. He was very fond of his young half-sister, and called her and Tim the heavenly twins.

'Have you spoken to Jenny?' The question was in-evitable, for Tim too often aired his grievances to Jenny's willing ear. 'If you tell Jenny and see what she says, then see Dom——'

'I've told her.'

Tim looked inconsolable and also a little sulky, Bryony noted with some surprise. He was good-look-ing, as their father had been, and rather wilful, which was a trait he had probably also inherited from

Rupert Charn, who had let little stand in his way when he really wanted something.

'And?' Bryony prompted him, letting a handful of glittering white sand run through her fingers while her blue eyes watched his face. 'What did she say you should do?'

'Think it over very carefully.' His slightly mocking imitation of his sister-in-law's gentle tones made Bryony frown; she liked Jenny. 'I don't know why I bothered; you know neither of them will go against Dom when it comes to the point!'

It was true, Bryony had to admit; she had suffered from the same sense of frustration herself on more than one occasion, and she had never become so involved in anything as Tim was at the moment. He often went with the schooners to Basse-terre, and it had been during one of these trips that he met and, so he claimed, fallen in love with a schoolteacher quite a number of years older than himself.

Dominic had declared him too young to know his own mind, and certainly too young to marry a woman of well over thirty, which was what he was anxious to do. Secretly Bryony had to agree with Dominic, although she would never have said so, for she was much too fiercely loyal to Tim.

'Would you like me to speak to him?'

Heaven knew what made her offer, for Dom was less likely to listen to her than to Jenny, but she had spoken impulsively, as she so often did, and she could not go back now. Besides which Tim, judging by his expression, seemed to think she had some chance of succeeding. He tapped his excellent teeth with a thumbnail as he considered for a moment.

'Would you, Bry?'

He must be fully aware of the fact that she already realised how rash she had been, but she shrugged and laughed, as if it worried her not at all. 'If you think it will do any good!'

Tim regarded her for a moment; a small slim figure in a blue cotton dress, her copper-red head bare because her wide-brimmed hat lay on the sand beside her. She was already pretty and would probably develop into a beauty in a very few years from now, but at the moment she had a childlike vulnerability that was very appealing, and Tim saw her from the masculine point of view and smiled.

'Oh, I think you could do a lot of good,' he told her. 'Just be sweet and nice, Bry, and he'll listen to you.'

Looking at him over her shoulder, Bryony pulled a face, tossing back the coppery hair in a gesture of unconscious defiance. 'I'm not sweet and nice, Tim, and I couldn't fool Dom into thinking I was, but I don't mind doing what I can to help.'

'Thanks! After all, I'm old enough to know my own mind and old enough to please myself who I marry—it isn't as if he has any right to put his foot down.'

'But you don't have the nerve to tell him so!' She could not resist the taunt, though she did not blame him in the least for feeling as he did.

The older he got the more darkly arrogant Dominic Laminaire became, and yet she knew he could be so gentle and understanding if he chose to be. He had insisted on sending her away to the English school in Dominica, but he had explained his reasons to her very patiently and kindly, and he welcomed her home each time she came with love and a genuine warmth, the memory of which she clung to all the weeks she was away.

'Do *you* have the nerve?'

Tim's grey eyes challenged her as he pushed himself up off the sand, and Bryony shrugged. She put her hands in his and let him pull her to her feet. Standing beside him made her appear even tinier, for both Rupert Charn's sons had inherited his lean height as well as his good looks. Brushing down her dress, she did not look at him when she answered. It was a question she had been asking herself during the past few minutes, but she shrugged with apparent carelessness.

'Why not?' she asked. 'He can't eat me!'

Dominic Laminaire was French. He had never absorbed the Englishness of his stepfather, nor his half-brothers who had both been educated at English schools in the islands. There was barely four years' difference in age between him and Jules, and yet somehow he always seemed so much more mature, for both Rupert Charn's sons had fair Anglo-Saxon colouring and boyishly good-looking features. Watching him through lowered lashes, Bryony thought no one, not even Dom himself, could claim he was good-looking.

He was tall and lean and had a craggy ruggedness that is sometimes much more attractive than mere good looks, and he was dark. His hair was not quite black, thick and very slightly curled, and his eyes were grey with thick short black lashes that quite often served to hide what was in his eyes, and he was tanned to a dusky gold that seemed to give truth to the Algerian pirate myth. He also had an earthy sensuality that Bryony found increasingly disturbing.

A plantation can be both hot and dirty, and Dominic showed signs of being both as he stood in the window with his back to the light, looking at Bryony. Perched on the very edge of his desk, she was wishing she had not made that rash promise to Tim to intervene on his behalf, and especially that she had not chosen to catch Dom when he came in from the fields. He was hot and tired and looked as if the last thing he wanted was to be appealed to by a young girl with obvious doubts about the cause she was pleading.

While she waited for his response, Bryony pondered on the man himself. He should have married long since and provided Petitnue with its next generation, but so far he had given all his energies to making the island pay its way as it never had before in its history, and to bringing up his young half-brother and Bryony, and sometimes she felt very sad about it.

She couldn't see his expression properly and she wished he would stand where she could judge him better. 'You're simply doing this because it's what Tim wants, aren't you, Bryony?'

He always put everything so neatly into a nutshell and made it sound far less important than it was. 'Tim's so unhappy, Dom. You have no idea how he feels.'

For a second only Dominic's wide and slightly crooked mouth tipped into a smile that gave a momentary gleam of warmth to his eyes too. 'Tim's feeling his feet—sowing his wild oats, or whatever other well-used adage you care to use. He thinks he's in love, and——'

'How do you know he isn't?'

She slipped the question in with breathless haste, and a frown flitted between black brows for a moment. 'At twenty? And with a woman of thirty-five? I doubt it, Bryony, I doubt it very much!'

'But you don't *know*! How can you know, you've never——'

She stopped there, aware that the grey eyes were watching her closely, waiting for her to complete that rash assumption, but she could not go on with it. She had never really known just what Dom's relations were with her own sex; he frequently visited other islands on business, but there was nothing to say he did not sometimes mix business with pleasure. It was a possibility that had not seriously occurred to her before, and she felt strangely and inexplicably embarrassed suddenly. The way he was looking at her now seemed to suggest it was very possible, and that made it worse.

'I'm sorry, Dom, I didn't mean to be——' She shrugged uneasily, then lifted her chin and tossed her coppery-red hair back over her shoulders in a gesture designed to challenge his opinion. 'But you should realise how Tim feels. He's your brother, and you should have a little sympathy with his feelings.'

'I have every sympathy with his feelings.' Dominic took a thin dark cheroot from a case and lit it, the flame of the lighter carving new dramatic lines on that craggy face while he bent over it. Then he blew smoke from his lips and looked across at her steadily. 'I simply cannot condone a hasty marriage by a boy who's scarcely out of school to a woman who is almost old enough to be his mother! In all probability that's what is behind all this, and I can sympathise to some extent. Mama died when he was born and he's never been coddled and spoiled by a woman—he's only had men to bring him up. He probably sees her as a mother figure and he's not old enough to tell the difference!'

'Oh, Dom, that's not fair!'

'Fair?' He mused on her accusation for a second, then shrugged as if he half admitted it. 'I'm being sensible, Bryony, that seems to me to be more important at the moment than being fair, if it means stopping him from doing something he'll most likely regret later on. You must see the sense of that, surely.'

So much of what he said was true, and Bryony hated to have to admit it, even to herself. But no matter what her common sense told her she was, as ever, guided by her heart, and she could not do an about-face and desert Tim's cause now. Feeling rather as if she had been backed into a corner, her instinct was to be defiant, and she got up from the edge of the desk and faced him.

'He could always just go away and get married without asking you, or saying anything about it at all, you know! And if he suggests it I shall encourage him!'

'Bryony!'

She had turned and was on her way to the door, but his voice had an edge that she recognised with a slight catch in her breath as she turned to face him once more. He ground out the cheroot in an ashtray on the desk, and she could not help watching the long hard strength of his fingers that crushed the thinly rolled tobacco into a heap of smoking shreds that smelled pungently in the small room. Having called her attention to him, he stood for a moment with a hand in his pocket and studied the smouldering mess in front of him.

'I hope you aren't thinking of doing anything silly, Bryony. I know Tim is old enough to please himself, but he's too young to tie himself for life to a woman so much older. I doubt if he really knows whether or not he's in love with her.'

'I believe he is!'

He shrugged his broad shoulders as if he doubted her conviction, but was willing to concede the vague possibility. 'If he is, then it won't hurt to wait a while, will it? True love doesn't wilt in the face of opposition, does it?'

Being asked to pass judgment on a subject she had to admit she knew virtually nothing about took her by surprise, and Bryony shook her head slowly, conscious of a flush of colour that was bound to be noted. 'I—I don't know, Dom—how could I?'

'How could you?' He repeated it softly, and Bryony noticed he was smiling, though it was a wry and rather tight smile that found no reflection in his eyes. 'When next you go into a huddle with Tim, suggest to him that he waits for a while—it can't hurt if it's the real thing, as he claims, and if it isn't—well, he'll give himself time to find out before it's too late. He'll know better, and be in a better position to support a wife, in a couple of years.'

'A couple of years!'

Dominic laughed. Shaking his head, he thrust both hands into his pockets and watched her with an expression in his eyes that was far too deep for her to understand. 'Does that seem such a long time to you, Bryony?'

'It's a long time to wait when you're in love with someone.' She caught the swift flick of one dark brow and hastily amended what she had said. 'At least I imagine it is.'

She noticed him looking at his watch, and he came round the desk, putting an arm about her shoulders as he led her to the door of his office. The arm was firm and warm on the coolness of her own skin through the thin cotton dress she wore, and he smelled of dust and heat and a masculine scent she had never noticed quite so strongly before.

'Don't let Tim involve you too deeply, Bryony. I know you two are closer than any of us, but I'd hate you to get caught up in something you can't handle.'

'I don't understand—what could I get caught up in?'

Across the hall she could see Marie from the corner of her eye, padding across the wooden floor from the kitchen to the dining-room, and the smell of *calalou* tickled her nostrils, tempting her appetite. Marie was an excellent cook in the best Creole style, and her crab soup was as good as any produced by a *Cordon Bleu* cook. She caught Dominic's eye and nodded, a signal he seemed to have no difficulty interpreting.

'It's almost time for dinner, Bryony, and we both have to get clean and tidy before we eat, so let's leave this for now, eh?' His arm was still around her shoulders while they mounted the wide staircase together, and when they reached her bedroom door he turned her to face him for a moment. His hands on her shoulders, he looked down into her face and half-smiled. 'You seem to have grown into a woman without me noticing it happen,' he confessed, and Bryony looked at the wide, sensual mobility of his mouth rather than meet his eyes.

'Maybe you just weren't looking,' she suggested.

'Maybe.' He seemed to make the admission reluctantly, and his strong fingers still rested on her shoulders until they squeezed lightly into her flesh before releasing her. 'Maybe so, *petite*, but I must take more notice from now on.'

From her window Bryony could see the other side of the island, for the house was built near the elongated tip and set on a slight hill that overlooked the lush greenness of trees and shrubs, with the sea just visible beyond them. Immediately outside her window and occasionally trespassing into her room, a bignonia displayed its bold orange trumpets as it twined its way over the side of the house, and beyond that, hibiscus in red, white and yellow ran riot with the star-shaped red and white blossoms of fragrant frangipani.

A huge jacaranda blocked her view to one side with its feathery fern-like leaves and blue flowers, and next to it an immortelle displayed its coxcombs against the deep blue Caribbean sky. This was the leisure part of the island, the house and gardens; it was the greater, wider part that supported them all and had kept the Laminaires prosperous for so long.

Beyond the gardens stretched the plantation with a forest of banana plants fanning their shredded leaves against the hot sky and beyond them again, Dominic's latest venture, a crop of low-growing pineapples. At the far side of the island, out of sight from her windows, was the village.

In the beginning it had been no more than mean

shacks that housed the imported slaves who worked the plantation, but now it was in fact a small village of neat little houses, each with its own patch of garden. Quite a few of the field workers had been born on Petitnue, although there was always a certain shifting element who came and went, and everyone knew that Laminaire paid well and looked after his workers.

Although not a native born, like Dominic, Jules and Tim, Bryony felt very much at home on the island after eight years, and she could not imagine anyone wanting to give up the life there, as it seemed likely Tim was going to do. He would miss Petitnue; he had been born there and, apart from his years in school, he had lived there all his life. Even at school he had come home for holidays and the one weekend a month, as she had done herself. He would surely miss it all.

Shaking off a mood of rather pessimistic gloom, she began getting ready for dinner with, somewhere in the back of her mind, a resentment against the woman who threatened to change all their lives if Tim persisted in his pursuit of her.

A lime green dress set off her red hair with dazzling effect, and showed off her bare, golden-tanned arms, and she used a new bottle of expensive French perfume that Tim had bought her, with a lavish hand. Somehow she had to put on a show and try to dispel her present mood.

It was her perfume that Dominic noticed first when she came down to dinner. He turned from the *dressoir* with a glass in each hand and handed her one as he wrinkled his nose appreciatively. 'Fabergé?' he suggested, and looked at her over the rim of his glass.

'Tim bought it for me, do you like it?'

She felt she had to challenge the hint of surprise she thought she detected in his remark, as if he had not thought of her using sophisticated perfumes before. There was a suggestion of a smile in his eyes that made her suddenly uneasy and she drank hastily from her glass to disguise it, catching her breath on the dryness of the aperitif.

'It's very—effective.'

He always seemed so very French when he used his hands like that, and she wondered just what he meant by effective. She had been over-generous with the perfume, she had to admit, and she realised suddenly that he might be thinking there was some ulterior motive behind it; that she had done it with some idea of making herself more attractive to him, and hoping to enlist his support for Tim.

The thought was so discomfiting that she walked away and stood looking out of one of the windows, across the gardens to the silky blue Caribbean. She had never before let herself dwell on things like that and she found it hard to believe she was doing it now. Dominic was—Dominic, her guardian and Tim's too, even though he considered himself beyond such guidance now. She had never before thought of him in any other light, and the fact that she did so now disturbed her.

'Tim isn't joining us for dinner, did you know?'

Turning quickly, she stared at him for a moment, unsure what he expected of her. She had seen Tim not long before she came back to the house, but he had said nothing to her about not being with them for dinner. It was rather late to be crossing to one of the other islands, but it was possible Tim did not see it the same way.

'I didn't know.'

'He didn't tell you?' He took a sip from his glass, watching as she shook her head. 'He's probably sulking; taken himself off somewhere to the other end of the island as a token of protest.'

'Maybe.'

'Marie says he let her know he wouldn't be in for dinner but didn't say why. I thought perhaps he might have told you.' He took another sip from his glass and Bryony caught a glimpse of a smile on his mouth a second before he put it to his lips. 'You usually know what he's up to.'

'Well, in this case, I don't.' He was probably right about Tim's whereabouts, she thought, and said so. 'He could be down with Louis, he was talking to him earlier and they looked to be pretty engrossed in something or other.'

'Oh?' A hint of narrowness gave his grey eyes a dismaying suggestion of cruelty, and Bryony wished she had not been so forthcoming. 'If Louis's encouraging him in his crazy romantic escapades, I'll flay him!'

The threat sounded far more fearsome than it was meant to be, she knew, but just the same Bryony felt a vague uneasiness when she remembered Tim talking so earnestly to Louis just after she left him. It would be just like Tim to think up some mad scheme for seeing his lady-friend, and to inveigle Louis into helping him to get to Guadeloupe; the two of them could handle the schooner between them in good weather.

'Louis wouldn't, Dom, he's too afraid of what you might do or say. Well,' she amended, unwilling to do

Louis the injustice of implying he lacked courage, 'at least he wouldn't like to go against you in something like that. He wouldn't, Dom.'

'He'd just better not!'

Louis was exactly Jules' age. He was Marie's grandson, born the exact same time that Louise Charn gave birth to Jules, only Louis had been born in one of the little houses down in the village. The result had been the same, for Marie's unmarried daughter had died when her son was born too, and Marie had brought him up. He would do anything for Tim or Bryony, for he had an almost fiercely protective attitude towards them. It was quite possible that Tim could persuade him to help in furthering his romantic plans, though Bryony prayed he hadn't.

It was with relief that she turned to speak to Jules when he came in to join them. Jules was simply an older version of Tim. The same fresh-faced look that belied his thirty years; tall and good-looking, just as their father had been. He made no pretence of doing other than dote on his pretty half-sister, just as Jenny, his wife, did.

After three years of marriage they still had no children, and it was an open secret that they both regretted it deeply. It was probably why they both cared so much for Bryony and treated her rather as if she was still a little girl, despite her eighteen years.

Jenny followed her husband into the room and came straight across to join Bryony by the window while Jules fetched them both an aperitif, murmuring something to Dominic as he did so. About Tim's absence, Bryony suspected, and glanced across at them uneasily.

Jenny was pretty in a rather gaunt way that was very English. Her short hair was brown, a rich golden brown that went with large and rather lovely hazel eyes and a wide mouth that smiled a lot, though with a hint of sadness sometimes. She liked living on the island, but sometimes Bryony thought she missed her friends and family in England. Hers and Jules' had been a holiday romance, begun while Jenny was staying with friends on Guadeloupe, and ending with her coming to Petitnue as Jules' bride only four weeks after they first met.

'Tim's gone missing.'

Jenny whispered the information with a hasty glance in Jules' direction as he made his way across the room with her drink, and Bryony nodded. As soon as he had gone back to continue his conversation with Dominic she went on, keeping her voice low, as if she did not want the two men to hear what she said, although almost certainly Tim was the topic of their conversation too.

'He's gone somewhere with Louis Ortega; Jules thinks they may have gone to Basse-terre to see that woman that Tim's been seeing, but I do hope he's wrong.'

All Bryony's loyalty to Tim welled up inside her at the breathless anxiety in Jenny's voice, because she knew just why it was that her sister-in-law hoped he wasn't seeing his schoolteacher. If Jenny had a drawback in Bryony's eyes, it was her sensitivity about offending Dom.

'I don't see why,' Bryony declared in a clear voice that easily reached the two men the other side of the room, and Jenny looked at her reproachfully. 'It's no one else's business if Tim's gone to see Sarah Bryant!'

'Is that her name?'

It was startling to realise how against the woman they all were without even knowing her name, and she wondered for a second if she had been too rash in mentioning her name within Dominic's hearing. 'She's a schoolteacher and Tim is a grown man, Jenny, not a boy! If he wants to see someone ten or fifteen years older than he is, then it's no one else's concern but Tim's! He's in love with her, so why shouldn't he go and see her?'

'Puppy love on Tim's side, surely, darling, isn't it?' Jules teased her gently, as he always did, not for a moment believing she could be as serious as she sounded. 'I suppose it *is* the same kind that makes the world go round!'

'Oh, you don't understand at all, do you?' It was so seldom that she had cause to cross words with Jules, and he looked quite startled for a second or two. 'You're as bad as Dom—he thinks it's all a five-minute wonder that Tim will grow out of! Doesn't it occur to either of you that he might *not* grow out of it?'

Dominic's normally pleasant voice was edged with a certain harshness that Bryony recognised as impatience, and he used his hands a lot in that expressive way he did. 'Bryony has become an expert in matters of the heart, Jules; sufficiently so to tell me how I should go about handling Tim's sensitive feelings in the matter of this schoolma'am he's infatuated with!'

'Oh, Dom, you're being cruel!'

Bryony's blue eyes reproached him, but he was apparently unrepentant, his gaze fixed on her steadily as he sipped the last of his aperitif. It made her uneasy and she was glad when he turned to put down his empty glass on the *dressoir* behind him.

'I don't claim to be an expert on anything,' she denied, clutching her own glass in tight fingers. 'I just think Tim should be free to make his own choice, that's all. You're too—too hard, Dom, you don't understand.'

'So you've informed me!'

The retort reminded her of that hastily recalled observation on his lack of experience, and she felt the colour in her cheeks as she sought consolation from her glass of bacardi. Almost inevitably it was Jules who came to her rescue, his laughter making light of the matter.

'Women always claim to be experts on *affaires de coeur*, Dom, don't you know that?' He gave no one a chance to follow up the question, but took his wife's arm and hugged her. 'And whether or not anyone else is hungry, I'm so ravenous I could eat Marie as well as the dinner she's got for us, so let's go in, shall we?'

Left alone with Dominic, Bryony gave him a brief, uneasy glance that evolved quite naturally into a deep and almost audible sigh of relief when he smiled. Taking her arm as they moved to follow Jules and Jenny, he squeezed the soft flesh of her upper arm with his strong fingers.

'I just wonder if Tim realises what a gallant little champion he has in you,' he said. 'Or if he deserves your blind devotion.'

'It isn't blind, Dom!' From below concealing lashes she looked at him anxiously, although she tried to disguise her anxiety. 'You won't flay him or Louis, will you, Dom?'

The threat had been no more than a figure of speech, of course, but somehow she had no difficulty picturing how different things would have been in the same situation only a few generations ago, with one of Dominic's ancestors making the same threat. There was still an element of savagery in Dom that she found disturbing. The Laminaires had created their own little world here on Petitnue, and she sometimes thought they had changed little when she looked at the latest of their line.

He curled his hard fingers about her arm and pulled her close for a moment, looking down into her face with eyes that gleamed like polished grey granite in his craggy face. 'Not while they have you for their advocate,' he promised, and sniffed appreciatively at the smells from the kitchen. 'Tim doesn't know what he's missing—smell that *calalou*! How could he forgo that for the sake of some——'

'Dom!'

'Ah!' He raised a hand and shrugged, then laughed as they went in to join Jules and Jenny. 'You will not let me forget, eh, *petite*? You are my conscience!'

CHAPTER TWO

IT was so dark that Bryony stirred only reluctantly, and noisy too, though it must be very late. She had come to bed just before midnight and had not meant to sleep until she heard Tim come in, but despite her good intentions, her body had eventually succumbed to a natural, healthy tiredness, and she had fallen asleep.

When she first woke it had been difficult to decide just what was causing the disturbance that had woken her. It was a strange and eerie howling, rising to a screech, and a rattle like stones on a tin roof, and it prodded relentlessly at her consciousness until she awoke; then she recognised it for what it was and sat up swiftly.

The banshee wailing of the wind and the curtains sweeping out into her room, billowing like full sails, even the bedclothes were shifting, it seemed, in the strong gusts from the partly open windows. It could only be a hurricane, or something close to it.

Only once before during her eight years in the islands had she been witness to the kind of fury these paradise islands could summon up, and it had frightened her so much that time that she had trembled for hours afterwards.

She was older now, and perhaps should have been less terrified, but even so her heart was thudding hard as she got out and reached for the robe that lay across the foot of her bed. Doing the commonplace things like putting on her slippers, automatically.

From inside the house came the bang of shutters being battened and the thud of hurrying feet on the stairs, voices; Jules' light baritone and Marie's sing-song Creole French as she spoke to Dom. And then it hit her with the force of a physical blow—she had not heard Tim come in! While she still coped with the sash at her waist she hurried across the room and just before she got there someone was hammering hard on her door.

She had not even time to open it before Dominic came in. He was still dressed, she noticed, and he looked so grim-faced that she said nothing, but watched while he reached out and after a running battle with the fury outside, pulled the shutters over her windows, muffling the sound of the wind and bringing a curious stillness into the room.

One glance at his face was enough to tell her that Tim had not come back and she put her hands over her mouth in sudden and sickening fear, staring at him over her finger-tips. For a moment, as he turned, the grim expression relaxed and he came to her, taking her hands in his and transmitting some of his own steadying strength to her, while he looked down into her face.

'It's all right, Bryony, don't look so scared. You've sat out one of these before, remember? Just after you came here first?'

It was ridiculous to say that her mouth was stiff, and yet that was exactly how it felt. Her lips had a curious numbness that made movement almost impossible, and yet somehow she managed to form the words she needed to say. 'Tim? Is Tim back?'

'No.' She knew he did not want to tell her, and there was something about the look in his eyes that made it hard for her to be calm. 'There was no warning of a hurricane, so that probably means it isn't going to last very long—it will probably blow itself out very quickly.'

'But they don't stand a chance!' She faced the worst, knowing it was what they could expect, but from somewhere Dominic found the wisdom and strength to shake his head and look as if he meant it.

'It depends where they were when it started, they could have been near enough to Petitnue to run for it before the worst hit them.'

'But if they're still in the passage——' The passage was a strip of water between two islands, notoriously rough going during a blow like this present one, and Tim and Louis were only two-handed.

'There's nothing we can do, kitten, except hope they aren't.'

The fact that he used her father's pet name for her was proof to Bryony's mind of how much he felt the frustration of his own helplessness, and she impulsively reached out and hugged close to his comforting strength, while his arms closed around her. With her face pressed close to his chest and her hands spread over his broad back she put everything out of her mind for just a few seconds, except the inexpressible sense of security he gave her.

Then he eased her away from him gently, his hands on her shoulders. 'I have to leave you, *petite*. There are the rest of the shutters to see to, and the quay to check, I can't leave it all to Jules.'

'Yes, of course—I'm sorry, Dom.' She left his arms reluctantly, but understood his reasons, and she looked up at him as she pushed back the thick untidy riot of red hair from her face. 'Is there something I can do?'

A momentary glimpse of a smile lightened his expression and showed warm in his eyes as he stroked back stray wisps of hair from her neck with an absently gentle finger. 'And get blown away in the wind?' He

put her away from him and walked back across the
room, turning in the doorway to consider for a
moment. 'If you really want to help, you can go and
sit with Jenny downstairs. This is her first experience
of this kind of thing and she's trying desperately to
keep her British stiff upper lip under control. Maybe
you can hold her hand until Jules can be with her.'

'Oh yes, of course, poor Jenny!'

Neither of them mentioned Tim again, but the dark
haunted look was back in Dominic's eyes again when
he strode off along the landing, and his mouth was a
firm straight line with thin lips. His feeling for Tim
went much deeper than he ever let anyone see, or so
Bryony believed, and with a stab of surprise she recognised how very much better she understood Dominic
than she had even a year ago.

She found Jenny in the *salon* alone, with the shutters
tight closed and the light burning with a fluttering
unsteadiness that suggested the power might fail at
any minute. Marie had only just left when Bryony
joined her, bringing the inevitable rum-based concoction to bolster their spirits; a recipe guaranteed to give
courage to even the faintest heart.

The room was big and seemed disconsolately empty
with only the two of them occupying it. It needed the
whole family to give life to its rather stiffly old-
fashioned comfort, and the screeching wind was too
suggestive of anguished loneliness as it tore at the
shutters and tried to wrench them open.

Jenny was fully dressed. Apparently she and Jules
and Dominic had stayed up for some time after she
went to bed herself, and she looked as if she was trying hard not to show how apprehensive she was.

Bryony found that her own natural jitteriness was mingled with a curious excitement, a reaction she did not quite understand, but which served to boost her courage.

'It's terrifying! I never realised it would be anything like this!' Jenny's voice was thinned by a shiver of fear and it was slightly unsteady; her sudden laughter served only to emphasise how she felt. 'Jules has told me about hurricanes, but I didn't—you *can't* imagine anything like this, can you?'

Prompted entirely by Dominic's expressed opinion, Bryony sought to reassure her. They sat side by side on the brocade-upholstered divan, and talking helped in part to distract the mind from the fury outside, although Bryony's ears were constantly attuned to the slightest sound that would suggest Tim was home.

'This isn't really a bad one, Jenny, and it will soon blow itself out, without doing too much damage, we hope.'

'I've seen newsreels and photographs—it can do a lot of damage, can't it?'

'It can cost the whole plantation,' said Bryony, 'if it goes on too long and is too severe, but Dom thinks it might not be too bad this time.'

'Houses too get blown away, I've seen them. The village houses seem so flimsy, in this wind——'

'They're a whole lot safer than this one would be if they collapse!' Realising how tactless that had been in the circumstances, Bryony hastened to amend the impression she had given. 'But I'm sure Dom's right—it isn't going to be a very bad one.'

They were talking much more loudly than they would normally have done, and keeping up the ex-

change simply to counter the din outside, and neither
of them mentioned Tim yet. Shutters banged somewhere inside the house, and Jenny jumped as if she
had been struck, then immediately laughed and shook
her head, looking at Bryony apologetically.

'I'm as jumpy as a kitten—I'm sorry, Bryony.'

'That's the last of the shutters battened.' Bryony
spoke as if she knew for sure. 'It keeps out some of the
noise as well as making it safer.'

It seemed so strange to think that she was the one
offering comfort to Jenny, and rather flattering that
Dom had thought her able to do it, when she thought
about it. She had not seen Jenny as a nervous woman,
and yet she was so obviously terrified in the present
situation.

'Now we all just sit it out?'

She was anxious to have Jules there too, Bryony
realised, and wished it was possible for Jenny's sake.
It had been a boost to her own courage to be close to
Dominic for those few seconds in her bedroom, and
she wondered if Jules had not taken time to offer
similar comfort to his wife.

'You and I sit it out,' Bryony said. 'Dom said
they'd be going down to check the quay next.' And to
see if Tim had come in yet, she knew, but did not say
so.

'In this?' Jenny looked appalled. She might not
have minded so much, Bryony thought, if Dominic
had taken the chance himself, but knowing Jules was
going with him gave her something else to fear.
'Bryony, they can't!'

'They won't if it isn't safe. The fact that Dom said
they were going means it *isn't* as bad as it sounds.

You know Dom wouldn't take unnecessary chances, Jenny.'

'No, of course he wouldn't.'

Bryony listened for the sound of the front door opening, and felt a great sickening lurch in her stomach when it happened. The storm had almost drowned the sound, but she was so alert to every sound that she heard it and Jenny did not. 'He wouldn't take any chances,' she echoed, for her own sake as much as Jenny's, and once more Jenny's thin, tremulous laugh fluttered across the muffled fury of the wind and rain.

'I'm sorry, Bryony, I'm being a real neurotic about this storm, aren't I?'

'No more than I was at first,' Bryony assured her without hesitation. 'I felt much better after Dom gave me a reassuring cuddle when he came to close my shutters.' Her own laughter was much more confident, and she pushed back her hair with one hand to cover a sudden inexplicable shyness. 'There's no one quite like Dom for inspiring confidence at times like this!'

'No, I imagine not.' For the first time Jenny's eyes showed interest in something other than the storm and the safety of her husband. She sipped the rum drink Marie had provided and looked at Bryony reflectively as the sweetened liquid slid silkily down her throat. 'I never realised quite how much store you set by Dom, until this moment,' she confessed. 'I always thought you—well, not actually disliked him, but resented his authority over you and Tim.'

Fingers curved about her own glass, Bryony shrugged. 'So I do most often, but he's very reassuring, for all that.'

'You're really quite close to him!'

In some curious way Bryony thought she sounded almost as if she disliked the idea. It was something she had never given a lot of thought to herself, and she found it discomfiting to do so now. Her deliberately careless shrug betrayed it.

'Dom and me? I don't think we are, Jenny; it's me and Tim that Jules calls the heavenly twins, isn't it?'

'Because you're much of an age, but you—depend on Dom an awful lot, I've noticed; it's being so much older, I suppose.' Jenny laughed and took another sip of her punch before admitting it. 'I suppose we all depend on him, come to think of it!'

'Dom *is* Petitnue!' Bryony made the declaration without any thought of being doubted, and Jenny was nodding thoughtfully. Laughing, Bryony spread her hands, unconsciously mimicking one of Dominic's gestures. 'I mean, he's the Laminaire, the rest of us are invaders in a way, aren't we?'

'Hardly that!' Jenny's face had a flush of warmth, though whether from the effects of the punch or not, it was hard to tell. 'Jules was born here!'

Resentment was something new too, and Bryony wondered if there were emotions hidden under Jenny's quiet exterior that only Jules knew about. She did not feel capable of putting Dominic's special position into words, but she felt she ought to try. There had never been any doubt in her own mind that Petitnue belonged to the Laminaires, even though her own father had worked it for years. She remembered the antagonism between her father and Dominic, and how strongly Dominic had felt about taking the running of the plantation out of his stepfather's hands. It had taken her father's death to solve that situation, and she dared not think what might have happened if Rupert Charn had lived on.

'Do you think Dom thinks of us as invaders?'

Bryony knew she should not have hesitated before she answered, but sometimes she did wonder if Dominic would have felt more in control of his own small kingdom if he did not have his secondary family there too. 'I don't think so.' She did not like to feel she was in any way resented by Dominic, for without Petitnue and the security it offered, she would feel like a ship without a rudder. 'Oh no, I'm sure he doesn't, Jenny!'

'He——' Jenny stopped, shaking her head as if she had had second thoughts. Then she looked up and half-smiled, shrugging her shoulders in a way she had learned from Jules. 'I've been living here for three years now, and I never—I don't seem to be able to get near to Dom.' She made the admission as if it was something she regretted very much, and Bryony nodded.

'Dom isn't an easy man to know,' she remarked, as if she had experienced the same frustration herself.

For the first time since Bryony came downstairs, they fell silent for a while, conscious of the wind and the rattling fury of the rain against the shutters. Then Bryony realised it was diminishing, gradually dying out, becoming less noisy and less overwhelming, and she looked at Jenny.

'It's blown itself out! Just as Dom said it would!'

She saw the brief closing of Jenny's eyes, as if she offered up a brief prayer, and then remembered Tim. Not that he had left her thoughts completely since it all began, but for a few moments at a time she had been able to put possible consequences to the back of her mind. Now she was once more reminded, and she got to her feet, swinging round quickly when the room door opened.

'Marie?'

'It's dyin', *petite*!'

Bryony listened to the howling wind, as it died slowly to a moan, giving up its strength like some dangerous monster with moans and cries. 'It's dying!' she echoed, and gave it a while longer.

Marie's round golden face had a slightly greyish tinge and her mouth was uncharacteristically tight-lipped. Her hair was greying, though not yet far enough to be called grey, and she carried herself with the inimitable grace of the Creole, despite her seventy years.

Five generations ago Marie's ancestors had been landed on this jewel of an island with no say in whether they wished to stay or not, but a great deal had happened in the time between, both to them and to Petitnue. African blood had mingled with French and the handsome progeny mixed in turn so that Marie as a girl had inherited a light golden-skinned beauty that typified the Creole. She was as much part of Petitnue's history as Dominic was, and they both recognised and acknowledged it.

The Laminaires had always spoken French, only the advent of Rupert Charn had introduced English to the island, but Marie spoke it well, better than most of the other inhabitants of Petitnue did. She also had her own strict protocol with regard to her employers. Dominic was undisputed master, being the only Laminaire, then Jules and Tim. The women were rarely consulted and Bryony least of all, so it was quite automatic for Marie to address herself to Jenny, even though she was the last newcomer.

'I go down an' see if the schooner come back, *maîtresse*—I won' be gone long.'

Taken by surprise, Jenny looked at her for a moment uncomprehendingly, but Bryony followed her meaning at once and turned to her eagerly, filled with a restless need to do something positive at last. 'That's a good idea, Marie! I'll go too, just as soon as I've put on some clothes!'

Clearly Marie had reservations about her going to the quay, and her dark eyes looked at Bryony as if she was still the small anxious girl who had arrived there eight years before. 'I don't know if I should let you go, Miss Bryony. If anythin' happen to you, I have Monsieur Laminaire blamin' me!'

'He won't blame you, Marie!' Bryony brushed aside her fears, wishing yet again that Marie did not see her as such a baby, unable to take care of herself. 'The wind's dropping all the time, and by the time I've changed my clothes it'll be as safe as houses out there!' She took Marie's plump hands and pressed them between hers. 'I must go, Marie, you know I must; to see what's happened to Tim. You know how I feel, with Louis out there as well—I must go.'

Louis was not only Marie's grandson, he was the sole reminder of her marriage to a Portuguese overseer during Dominic's grandfather's time. Her only child had died giving birth to Louis and he was the zenith of her heaven; Bryony could guess how she was feeling, and she pressed the plump dark hands once more persuasively.

'You must understand, Marie.'

'*Mais oui, mon enfant, je comprends!*' Marie always spoke in French when she was emotional, and there were bright tears standing in her eyes when she turned away, a hand brushing across her face.

'Don't wait for me, I know you're anxious.' Bryony looked across at Jenny still seated on the divan. 'You'll stay here and wait, Jenny?'

'Can I do anything to help if I come?' Bryony shook her head and smiled ruefully. 'Then I'll stay here and wait for Jules. Dom might not take kindly to having us both under his feet if he's busy down there!'

That was something Bryony preferred not to comment on. She simply waved a hand and followed Marie out of the room. 'You set on goin'?' Marie demanded, and Bryony nodded without stopping to argue the point, running upstairs as quickly as her long robe allowed, and Marie shrugged, then slipped out of the front door into the tail of the storm.

The bedroom seemed horribly stuffy with the shutters closed, but she hesitated to open them again yet; the wind was still high enough to be troublesome, apart from the fact that it would all take time and she wanted to hurry. There might or might not be news down at the quay, but at least she would not be sitting and waiting, feeling maddeningly helpless because there was nothing she could do.

She dressed quickly and with no thought to how she looked. She pulled on a pair of jeans and a shirt, then tied a scarf Madras fashion around her head and tucked in the ends, as the island girls did. Sliding her feet into leather casuals, she hurried back downstairs, looking in on Jenny again before she went out.

'I won't be long, Jenny, and I'll tell Jules to come as soon as he can, O.K.?'

'I'll be glad to see him safely back,' Jenny confessed,

then bit anxiously on her bottom lip. 'I do hope Tim's safe, Bryony, Jules will be shattered if anything's happened to him.'

'So will Dom!' Heaven knew why she made that swift, defensive statement, and she caught Jenny's raised brow as she turned away. 'I'll see you, Jenny!'

Marie was already gone, and Dominic and Jules would have taken the jeep, but she knew her way around the plantation blindfold and she did not hesitate to take a short cut through the dark wet groves. It was a little more than three kilometres to the quay from the house, but she had taken longer walks than that many times and the prospect did not deter her until she stepped outside.

The wind had abated considerably, but it was still strong enough to make walking against it a breathtaking and vigorous exercise, and the darkness gave a sense of endlessness to the long path from the gardens to the groves. Despite the temptation offered by the road that circuited the perimeter of the island, she still took the track through the tall plants, even though she regretted it almost as soon as she started.

It was too dark to see much, but a sliver of moon came out from behind the clouds as she made her way through, and she could see that this part at least was virtually undamaged by the storm. Maybe around the edges, where the full force of the wind could touch them, the story might be different, but here the huge ragged leaves of the bananas still fanned out against the night sky, glossy and heavy with rain, and shushing eerily in the wind.

One thing she had not allowed for in taking the track instead of the road was the soaking the ground had received, and she slipped and slithered on the un-accustomed mud. Confident of her direction, she branched off and heaved a sigh of relief to see the lights at the far end of the track, hurrying towards them as fast as the treacherous ground allowed.

The village had suffered very little damage consider-ing its position and the light construction of the houses, but here and there a shutter hung awry, flapping des-pondently in the dying wind, and the women stood in gossipy little groups with the children around them, wide-eyed at being awake at the unfamiliar hour. Bryony was recognised and acknowledged with the un-failing courtesy of the West Indian as she enquired after everyone's well-being, dark faces splitting into dazzling smiles, even in this situation.

A fallen palm leaned drunkenly across the rough track road, and she eyed it warily before venturing to duck underneath it and carry on down to the quay. The sheds were ablaze with lights, so obviously none of the island's power supply had suffered damage, and the last squalling cries of the wind were almost drowned by the babble of human voices.

What Bryony searched for as she walked down on to the broad concrete loading quay was the second schooner; the *Bonne Chance*, praying that her name had been an omen in this instance. Her sister ship, the *Félicité*, was at her customary mooring, apparently none the worse after the storm, but she could see noth-ing yet of the *Bonne Chance*, and her heart thudded urgently as she approached a group of men loading piles of boxes and bags back on to a truck.

'Have you seen Mr Laminaire?'

They must have seen him, of course, but there was

no sign of Dominic at the moment. One of the older men gave her a smile, one hand indicating the direction of the house and the road. 'He gone back to the house, *maîtresse*; Monsieur Jules too.'

With bad news? Bryony wondered, and once more glanced across at the *Félicité* riding the still heavy swell at her mooring. 'The *Bonne Chance*, has she——?'

'She come up in *crique*, *maîtresse*. Not much broken,' he added cheerfully, and Bryony knew he would never have looked so cheerful if anything had happened to her two-man crew. They were sensitive people and very fond of her young half-brother, as they were of her.

'And the two men—— What about my brother and Louis Ortega? Were they all right?'

'Li'l bit hurt, not bad.'

It was assurance enough, and Bryony nodded her thanks, turning back without asking how much damage had been done to the quay and its buildings—property did not matter so much. She wanted to get back and see Tim; discover for herself how little or how much he had been hurt.

She had noticed Louis Ortega's little house in darkness as she passed, so obviously he had been taken up to the house as well, so that Marie could take care of him, and since she had seen nothing of Marie either, she had probably returned with them in the jeep. Marie would not soon let her precious grandson out of her sight again, now that she had him back.

Returning through the towering jungle of banana plants, Bryony made her way cautiously, even though the wind had already started to dry out the ground. The path was still slippery and offered a very precarious footing in the almost dark, so that she began once more to wish she had taken the road instead.

Seeking a drier section, she choose to walk along the edges of the rows of plants, but found the large ragged leaves constantly across her path, and she muttered a mild curse when the scarf was snatched from her head. It hung suspended just out of reach, flung there by the spring-back of a branch, and it was pointless to try and recover it, so she went on, her hair tumbled by the still frisky wind.

Taking the path to the house once more, she noticed that the shutters had been opened again. Lighted windows beamed out across the wet gardens, striking splashes of colour on heavy-headed blossoms and glinting with swiftly gone flashes of diamond brightness on wet leaves. The ground smelled lush and cool, and she could almost hear the sound of the thirsty soil drawing in the fresh rainfall.

Jenny was in the hall when she walked in, apparently having just come downstairs, and Jules came out from the *salon* in the same instant. Looking at Bryony's rumpled and untidy red head and the mud on her shoes, he grinned ruefully.

'What happened to you, sweetheart? You look as if you've been through a hedge!'

'I've been through the groves.' She glanced from him to Jenny, seeking some clue to the way things were, then beyond him to the stairs. 'How's Tim? I was told he wasn't badly hurt.'

Jules put an arm about his wife's shoulders and smiled. 'He's got a couple of broken ribs and some hefty bruises, but he isn't too bad; Marie's strapped him up as well as she can until we can get the doctor over tomorrow.' He looked at her curiously, a brow raised. 'Is Dom putting the jeep away?'

Bryony frowned, suspicion niggling uneasily at the back of her mind. 'Isn't he here? I was told he drove back to the house with you.'

'So he did,' Jules agreed, 'but when we got back and found you'd gone off somewhere on your own, he went out again to find you.' He eyed her dishevelment and grinned. 'If you came through the groves no wonder he missed you. He isn't going to be very pleased, Bryony, he told you to stay put, didn't he?'

'He can hardly *tell* me to do anything, Jules—I'm old enough to act on my own initiative!'

Jules regarded her for a second, one brow slightly raised and a deep and speculative look in his eyes. 'I'm not sure that Dom shares your view, sweetheart, and he was pretty wild when he went out again.'

'Oh.'

She could sense that curiously apprehensive manner of Jenny's, and guessed that she was thinking along the same lines. If Dominic had gone back for her he was not going to be very pleased, as Jules said, but she could not have guessed he would go looking for her. Shrugging carelessly, she threw off any vague feeling of uneasiness she felt.

'Oh well, he'll realise I'm not on the road before he gets very far.'

There was more bravado than carelessness behind it, and Jules realised it, cocking a brow at her he pulled a face. 'You were told to sit tight with Jenny, I understand. The fact that you went plodding around in the mud instead isn't going to make you the most popular girl in town, darling, and you know it isn't just because you didn't do as you were told. You could have got yourself into a pretty tricky situation if that wind had got up again while you were out in the groves.' .

'But it had dropped by the time——'

'And it could have got up again just as quickly, Bryony, and you know it.'

It wasn't like Jules to scold her, and she felt very chastened as she offered her explanation. 'I couldn't just sit and wait when I didn't know what had happened to Tim; Dom must have realised that.'

She spun round quickly when she heard the jeep pulling up on the drive outside, and it was both instinctive and unconscious when the tip of her tongue flicked briefly across her lips when she heard the door slam shut. Dominic came up the front steps in one stride, his whole bearing giving away the black mood he was in as well as the dark brows drawn together and the stony hardness in his grey eyes.

He came straight across to where the three of them stood grouped near the foot of the stairs, but it was Bryony who had his attention. 'Where the devil did you get to?' he demanded. 'I tracked you through that damned mud and found this on one of the plants!' He thrust her head-scarf into her hands and she took it automatically. 'Damn it, Bryony, why don't you do as you're told just for once—why didn't you stay home with Jenny?'

'Because I went to see what had happened to Tim, of course!'

Her response was hasty and slightly breathless, and there was a flush in her cheeks aroused by the same emotion that made her eyes so huge and brightly blue.

She heard Jenny's sharply indrawn breath and vaguely registered irritation, but her eyes were fixed on Dominic. He looked dark and stormy and dangerously near to losing his temper, and she really didn't want that to happen; especially when she recognised the grey tinge of tiredness below his tan.

'I've spent quite enough time tonight chasing around after you two!' He waved a large hand in a curiously violent gesture. 'For two people who claim to be adult, you both behave with incredible stupidity and I've a good mind to wash my hands of the pair of you!'

'I wish you would, then we'd both be able to live our lives *our* way!'

The words were cut off sharply when she gasped in surprise at the stinging slap to her cheek, and she once more registered Jenny's swiftly drawn breath. One hand to her face, she stared after Dom's angrily striding figure as he started upstairs, taking the wide steps two at a time and each step thudding hard with fury on the wooden stairs.

She stepped back quickly when Jules reached out and took her hand, his face showing regret rather than sympathy, so that she could not help feeling he did not blame Dominic for what he did.

'Don't think too badly of him, Bryony.' She turned and looked at him with blankly empty eyes for a moment, then shook her head slowly. 'He's had a pretty hard time tonight, and finding you gone was the last straw. You know how explosive he gets when his emotions are involved.'

'His—his emotions?' She looked at Jules, the blankness in her eyes becoming increasingly curious. 'Are you saying that Dom——'

'I'm saying it's time Dom got married and found himself a wife to occupy his time.' He pulled Jenny close to him and kissed her forehead, smiling down into her eyes. 'It works wonders at putting business worries into perspective—Dom doesn't allow his emotions enough rein, and I'll be glad if he would! If ever he finds himself worrying about one of us, and you in particular, being his ward in a manner of speaking, he can't cope with the havoc it plays with his cool practicality.' He kissed Jenny on her mouth and laughed. 'I'll have to see if I can't find him someone like Tim's schoolteacher, eh, darling?'

He turned and drew Jenny with him towards the stairs, looking back over his shoulder at Bryony. 'I'm coming in a minute,' she said, and he nodded.

The wind had dropped and there was only the familiar soft noises that every night brought to the old house, but Bryony was restless, too restless to think of going back to sleep, and she wandered back into the *salon*. Standing by the windows, she looked out into the garden for a moment or two, then walked over and switched off the lights, to give the thin sliver of moon a chance to show itself in long threads of silver across the floor.

Tim would be asleep, lulled by one of Marie's secret recipes for healing sleep, and Marie would probably be alert to the slightest sound from her precious grandson. She thought of Tim and his schoolteacher, of Jules and Jenny, happy and wrapped up in each other's company—in love.

Dominic should have married before now. He must surely have met women who would have been willing enough to become his wife and share his small kingdom with him, but he had never, so far as she knew, found the one he was looking for. If he did—— She moved away from the window and made her way back to the hall and the stairs. If he did she didn't think she could go on living on Petitnue—it would not be the same, and she hated to think of it changing. Tomorrow he would say he was sorry—she knew Dom.

CHAPTER THREE

BRYONY had thought she would be too restless to go back to sleep after the events of the night, but no sooner had she put her head on the pillow than she was asleep, and it was well past her usual time when she woke. Her room was bright with morning light when she opened her eyes and the perfume of the frangipani drifted in from the gardens, enhanced by last night's rain.

She stretched lazily, taking a few minutes to remember exactly what had happened last night that had stunned her with its unexpectedness, and almost unconsciously a hand strayed to her left cheek. There was nothing to show it this morning, but she could still recall the shock of realising that Dominic had actually struck her.

All the time she was bathing and dressing she mused on what he was going to say to her this morning, for she had no doubt at all that he would apologise. What she found curious was how unwilling she was to think of him asking her forgiveness. Apologising never came

easily to him, and in her own case she felt herself oddly
in sympathy with his impulsive violence.

She must see Tim this morning too, as soon as she
was dressed, and find out for herself how much he was
hurt. He would be anxious, she thought, to know that
she was on his side, and she wished she felt more in
sympathy with him and less with Dominic. It had been
simply defiance that made him do as he did, almost certainly, but she wished he hadn't involved Louis as well.

At some time during the last century the original
house had been extended and a whole new wing built in
a T-shape across the old one, and it was in the old part
of the house that Marie had her room, the rest of the
rooms being kept for the very occasional visitor. It was
when Bryony was passing across the landing going towards Tim's room that she saw Louis Ortega coming
from one of the spare rooms, and she stopped, looking
along at him while he closed the bedroom door.

He had a piece of strapping across the top of one
arm and a dark bruise down one side of his face, and
when he looked up and saw her he hesitated. Perhaps
it was the unexpectedness of seeing her that confused
him, for he had no shirt on and the light slacks he wore
were torn and crumpled, his once white plimsolls
stained with sea-water. He was never anything other
than neat and clean and his present dishevelment obviously made him self-conscious for a moment.

'Good morning, Louis, how are you?'

The fact that she stood waiting for him gave him
little option but to join her, but he came along the
corridor with such an air of discomfiture that Bryony
was tempted to find it amusing. It was difficult to
believe sometimes that he and Jules were the same age,

for Louis Ortega had an air of maturity about him, even in his present situation, that Jules lacked.

He was bigger than Jules too, not so much taller as much broader and, thanks to his unknown father, he was darker than Marie's light gold colour, with a skin like brown satin. Bryony's first sight of him had been when he lifted her out of the boat that had brought her to Petitnue when she was ten years old. She had been half asleep then and he had seemed strange and foreign and rather terrifying as he carried her ashore, and she had been frightened to death of him.

Since then he had become a good friend, acting as a kind of unofficial bodyguard to both her and Tim, as well as teaching Bryony the names of all the strange and exotic plants around her new home, and showing her the weird and beautiful things that grew beneath the deep blue waters of the Caribbean. How to swim and dive, and how to avoid the few unpleasant creatures that shared their island paradise. There was little he would not do for her or Tim, and she could guess that was how he had become involved with Tim in last night's affair, so that she smiled at him as he came to join her.

'Good morning, *maîtresse*. I'm sorry for the way I look, but I lose my shirt in the *crique* las' night when we go aground.'

Taking note of the strapping on his arm and the bruises, she looked sympathetic. 'Should you be around —are you all right?'

A wry smile suggested that her concern had not been shared by others, and she wondered whether it was Marie or Dom he feared most. 'Grand'mère don' believe in stayin' in bed when you ain't bad hurt!' He pulled a face and put a hand to his bruised cheek. 'I ain't hurt bad, *maîtresse*, on'y a cut an' some bruises, but I hurt some.'

Bryony shivered in sympathy, remembering the fury of last night's storm. 'I can imagine—I wonder you weren't both killed!'

Only in the past few months had he started to address her as mistress instead of using just her christian name as he had always done before, and Bryony suspected that it was Dominic's doing. She was growing up, and Dom was not the kind of man to take chances on familiarity breeding, if not contempt, at least too much familiarity. Occasionally Louis forgot and when he did she never commented, any more than Louis had commented on the reason for the change, but simply made it a habit.

She started along the landing once more and Louis fell into step beside her. 'Is Tim as lucky as you? Or did he get the worst of it?'

Louis's smile showed white in his dark face and he looked as if he anticipated her response without being unduly troubled by it. 'Oh, Tim got the worst! When we brought up in the *crique* I landed on top him an' broke he ribs!'

'Oh, Louis!' Reproach mingled with laughter in her eyes, for she could imagine Tim's language when he found himself pinned down by Louis's not inconsiderable weight, and he would never have found it amusing if Tim had not come off fairly lightly. Outside Tim's bedroom door she turned and looked at him. 'I doubt if Tim is finding it very funny; are you coming in to see him?'

A thumb scratched thoughtfully at Louis's black hair as he tried to judge what she wanted his answer to be.

'You think I be allowed?' he asked, and Bryony's eyes challenged him.

'Why not? Are you scared of what he'll do to you for falling on top of him?'

'I'm thinkin' of Monsieur Laminaire,' Louis returned swiftly.

'Dom will be having his breakfast by now, or he might even have already gone out, it's pretty late.' She tapped on Tim's door and waited for the familiar voice to invite her in, looking at Louis over her shoulder. 'Come in and see him, Louis—he'll be glad to know you're not too badly hurt.'

The smile she wore as she opened the door trembled away when she saw Tim, and she stopped so short in the doorway that Louis almost collided with her as he followed her in. She was not quite sure what she expected, but certainly not the pale face and dark-circled eyes that looked across at her, and she hurried over to him after her initial hesitation, and stood beside the bed, a strange chokey feeling in her throat suddenly. She had never seen Tim laid low before, and she found it alarmingly affecting.

'Oh, Tim!' Impulsively she crouched down beside him and took the hand nearest to her in both hers. 'I didn't realise how bad you were!'

Tim's head rolled side to side on the pillow and he was smiling, even though it had a slightly rueful look to it. 'Actually I don't feel too bad now, thanks to some foul-tasting voodoo juice that Marie's been dosing me with.'

'Same as I got!' Louis's voice was round with laughter, and Bryony looked up at him standing just behind her. 'But it good stuff, Tim, an' it Grand'mère's secret dose!'

'You deserve it!' Tim was more cheerful than she expected in the circumstances, although something told Bryony that quite a lot of this *bonhomie* was bravado. 'Did that great lump tell you that he knocked me flying when we went aground, and then fell on top of me?'

'He told me,' Bryony said. 'He says you've got broken ribs, Tim.'

'That's right, I came home last night in the jeep tied up in strips of Louis's shirt. I'm lucky it wasn't worse after the fall I took, and now I'm lying here in agony while he gets off with a few bruises!'

'Well, it's probably a judgment on you for giving us all such a worrying time last night—we were all worried sick about you, Tim.' It was the nearest she meant to get to reproaching him, but somehow she kept remembering Dominic's face last night; grey with anxiety and fatigue, and she *did* blame him. 'We didn't even know for sure where you were.'

'Couldn't you guess?' The edge of defensiveness on his voice betrayed the nervousness he felt beneath the determinedly bright exterior. 'Surely Dom knew, or guessed, where I'd gone, didn't he?'

Neither she nor Louis answered him, but Bryony changed the subject. 'It was very short-lasting, that's one blessing,' she said. 'Dom said it wasn't going to be a bad one, and it wasn't.'

There was a slight curl on Tim's top lip, she noticed uneasily, and from his eyes it was clear he suspected where her loyalties lay. 'Dom *would* be right, you should expect that, Bry—he always is, isn't he?'

She took a moment, wishing she could understand

him in his present mood as well as she had always thought she did. 'Tim, that isn't quite fair.' At her soft-voiced reproach, Louis shifted uneasily behind her, and she guessed he was reminded of the fact that he would inevitably be called upon to explain his own part in the expedition.

Tim looked unrepentant, and still determinedly cocksure. 'You must all have known where I'd gone, surely?'

Shrugging, Bryony let the matter slide without answering him, looking down at the hand she held. 'It's a relief to know you're not badly hurt, anyway. Does it hurt much?'

'It hurt like hell last night!' Tim declared bluntly. 'But this morning I'm more hungry than hurt, and all I've been given apart from that muck that Marie brought me is baby food. See what you can do about wangling me something a bit more substantial, will you, Bry?'

'I'll see what I can do.' She got up and stood beside the bed, her eyes thoughtful. 'Maybe you'll be able to come down later—Dom's sent for the doctor to come and see you, so he might say you'll be as well up and about.'

'What the hell did he want to do that for?'

'Because it's the most sensible thing to do!' Dominic had come into the room without anyone hearing him, except possibly Louis, who looked suddenly uneasy and glanced hastily at the door. Dominic loomed large and dark in the bright room, and he glanced only briefly at Tim, then shifted his gaze to Bryony. 'And I suggest it's too early in the day for you to have a room full of visitors.'

'I just called in on my way down!' The response was irresistible, and the merest flick of one dark brow recognised the fact resignedly.

'Your breakfast is waiting for you if you want any this morning; and when you've had *your* breakfast, Louis, I'll see you in my office!' As if he considered them both dismissed, he turned back to Tim. 'From the look of you it's as well that Doctor Gernais will be here some time after lunch. I think you'd better try and get some more sleep and give those ribs a chance to heal.'

'I'll see you again later, Tim.'

She lingered deliberately, aware that Louis had already left the room, discreetly soft-footed and offering no argument, and Dominic's glance fell on her again. 'I'll join you for breakfast in a few minutes, Bryony, don't wait for me.'

It surprised her that he had not already breakfasted, but she did not remark on it. Instead she simply nodded, gave Tim a smile that intimated some kind of conspiracy, and left. Usually Jules and Jenny were there for breakfast too, and they would take the edge off that stern and sober mood of Dom's.

Down in the hall she found Louis hovering around at the foot of the stairs and apparently waiting for her, and when she smiled at him curiously, he glanced hastily up the stairs behind her before he said anything. Checking to make sure Dominic was not following her, she suspected, and wondered what he had in mind.

'Tim promised to see her today, *maîtresse*, what happen now?' He kept glancing upstairs all the time and spoke low as if he feared he might be overheard. 'After las' night she maybe think he drowned.'

'Sarah Bryant?'

'Tim's woman.' He knew no name, apparently, or else he preferred not to say it aloud. 'She 'spect to see him today an' after that storm las' night——'

Bryony put herself in Sarah Bryant's place and could guess how she must be feeling this morning, if she was as fond of Tim as he was of her. 'She'll be worried about him. Louis, are you going out today?'

Louis was eyeing her in a way that suggested he knew what she had in mind. 'I got some work to do on the *Bonne Chance*, *maîtresse*, she got broke up a li'l.'

'But you could put one of the other men on to it, and go with the *Félicité*, couldn't you? Do you know what Miss Bryant looks like, or where to find her?'

He was cautious, and it wasn't like him to hesitate when Tim's happiness was involved. He must be very anxious about Dominic's reaction to last night, and she could not help but feel for him. 'I see her once, mebbe twice, *maîtresse*, but I don' know her, an' I——'

'You could find her and speak to her, let her know that Tim's all right, Louis.'

'Oh no, Bryony!' In his agitation it was more natural for him to let slip her christian name, and he was shaking his head firmly. 'I'm in trouble enough with Monsieur Laminaire, I ain't goin' to make no more!'

'But someone has to let the poor woman know, and I can't telephone from here without Dom finding out!'

'An' I can't go makin' trips to Basse-terre instead of mendin' broken spars without Monsieur Laminaire findin' out, *maîtresse*!'

'It was Bryony just now!'

'*Maîtresse*.' He persisted with the formality because, she suspected, it set him a little further apart from her.

'I can't get in no more trouble from Monsieur Laminaire! I tol' you 'bout Tim's woman so you could mebbe think of some way to let her know, but I can't take no more chances. Monsieur Laminaire skin my hide if I take messages 'stead of doin' my job!'

'Oh, Louis, you know that isn't true!'

'I can't do it, *maîtresse!*'

Reproach would do no good, Bryony recognised that; not even for Tim would Louis chance bringing down Dominic's wrath on his head again, and she heaved a great sigh of resignation. 'All right, Louis, I'll think of something.'

He was half-turned towards the kitchen door when he hesitated and looked back at her with dark, anxious eyes, asking for her understanding. 'I don' like sayin' no to you, *petite maîtresse*, but you know how Monsieur Laminaire is.'

'It's all right, Louis!' She made a wry face, touching his arm lightly with her finger-tips. 'I know just how Monsieur Laminaire is.' Once more she remembered that impetuous slap stinging her cheek, and shook her head. 'I'm not anxious to cross him again just yet either; but I'll think of something.'

When Dominic appeared at the top of the stairs, Louis edged nearer to the kitchen door, his voice dropped to a whisper. 'Take care, *petite!*' he warned.

Uncertain whether she should wait for Dominic to join her so that they could go in to breakfast together, Bryony hesitated long enough for it to have looked too pointed if she turned away then, so she stood watching him with a curious sense of anticipation as he came downstairs.

A blue shirt that showed a dart of brown throat at

the open neck and light fawn slacks gave him a deceptively casual air that Bryony did not take at face value. She judged instead by his eyes and the way he held his head, so arrogant and sure of his authority—the signs she had learned by experience to look for. He came down into the hall, and long smooth strides brought him across to her, steady grey eyes noting the flush in her cheeks and the slightly anxious way she watched him.

'Aren't you hungry this morning? I thought you'd be in having your breakfast by now!' He sounded cool and easy, but she saw the way he glanced briefly at the kitchen door, picking up, as she did herself, the tangled sounds of Creole that suggested Marie and her grandson were both talking at once. 'Or did you get held up?'

His meaning was obvious and Bryony saw no reason to hide the fact that she had stopped to talk with Louis. 'I was having a word with Louis—he's worried about Tim.'

A ghost of a smile tugged briefly at Dom's wide mouth, but did not reach his eyes. 'It's a pity he didn't worry a little more before he went off with him on that mad scheme last night. Then neither of them would have been feeling so sorry for themselves this morning!'

'They weren't to know it would blow up a storm— you said yourself there was no warning!'

'It's foolhardy to start a twenty-mile crossing at that time of day whatever the weather—and Louis should have known better, even if I can't expect Tim to have that much sense!'

'So you're blaming Louis?'

'I'm blaming him *and* Tim! I know Louis dotes on the pair of you, but if he'd had half the sense I've always credited him with, he'd have come to me when that trip was first proposed.'

'He couldn't!' He led her across the hall with a hand on her arm while she sought for words to remind him yet again that neither she nor Tim were children any longer. 'Tim isn't a baby, Dom, he's a man, and as a member of the family he has some authority! He had the right to go off if he wanted to, and Louis could hardly còme running to you as if Tim was still a school-boy bent on mischief!'

'That cry yet again!' The tightness of his grip made her wince and he immediately eased it when he realised he was hurting her. 'Why is it always the same complaint, Bryony? It would make more sense if you behaved as adults, but when Tim indulges in a silly—calf-love antic like last night it only helps to show how immature he is!'

'Dom, you must——'

'No, Bryony! I've had more than enough!' He silenced her firmly, and she subsided more from instinct than inclination as he saw her seated at the table. 'We'll have breakfast and then I have to give my attention to the business I'm supposed to be running here! You and Tim may do as you please without hindrance from me in future; you're free to do exactly as you like and with none of what you obviously consider is interference on my part!'

'Oh, Dom!' She scarcely noticed that they were alone in the room apart from Marie. Her eyes were suspiciously bright and she felt as if tears were not far off as she looked at him. 'I didn't want you to feel like that, I didn't mean to——'

'You have things your own way at last, Bryony, let that be an end of it!'

He looked so distant, and there was an unfamiliar coolness to the way he ignored her when she looked at him, that she wanted to do something about it. Instead she refused the food Marie brought for her and sat with a cup of coffee between her hands while he ate, his appetite apparently unimpaired. Remembering how she had expected him to apologise for last night, a small niggle of resentment stirred in her as she sat silent and unhappy while he scanned some letters beside his plate.

'Dom——'

He looked up, eyes cool and steady as far as she could tell for the shadowing lashes that made it difficult to be quite sure. He put down the letter he had been reading while she sought desperately for the right words, now that she had his attention. Then he reached out suddenly and covered her hand, strong brown fingers gently enfolding hers, holding them tightly for a moment before he said anything.

'I had meant to say I am sorry for last night,' he said, and his voice had a quiet softness that made the threatening tears even more imminent. 'I have never slapped you before, have I, Bryony?' She shook her head and briefly his mouth curved in to a smile, softening the lines of sternness and warming his eyes. 'Perhaps I should have done so more often when you were small, although I have never believed that devils can be beaten out!'

Her lower lip trembled unsteadily and she looked at him with a bright glistening look, unable to understand the way she felt. 'I never knew you thought of me as a devil. I—I didn't think I was as bad as that.'

'Only when you let that carroty head run away with your common sense,' he said, and shook his head. 'No matter, Bryony, I should not have struck you and I'm sorry I did. For one thing because it showed a sad lack of control on my part, and for another because I know how often you say and do things that infuriate me, without stopping to think. You speak first and think later—too late sometimes! You don't mean them, but it's too late to recall them!'

It was quite an unconscious gesture when she put a hand to her face, and she realised suddenly how unutterably relieved she felt to have some trace of normality restored between her and Dominic. 'I'm impulsive,' she allowed with a ghost of a smile. 'It's a trait shared by all the Charns.'

Dominic smiled, the letters beside him forgotten for the moment. Picking up his coffee, he rested his elbows on the table and gave her his whole attention. 'It does seem to be a family trait,' he agreed. 'Your father was here only a few weeks before he and Mama were married, and he married your mother only ten months after Mama died, and only six weeks after he met her. Jules knew Jenny only a month before they were married, and now Tim goes off after his——' He shook his head and laughed shortly. 'Yes, you could say that the Charns are impulsive!'

'Unlike the Laminaires?' She held his eyes for a long moment, her pulses racing with a kind of excitement she could neither control nor account for. 'You're not likely to go off and marry someone on the spur of the moment, are you, Dom?'

He took a sip from his cup and said nothing for a

moment, then she noticed a small and oddly disturbing smile on his mouth as he looked at her. 'I might surprise you one day, *petite*; but one thing I can promise you—my wife won't be someone I've known for barely a month, nor will I ask her to marry me until I'm quite sure not only that she's right for me, but that I'm right for her. I shall take the matter of her happiness very seriously'.

The fact that he had not denied he had marriage plans surprised her initially, until she realised it really should not have done. She stared at him for a moment, not knowing quite what to say. 'And *your* happiness, Dom? What about that?'

He smiled. 'Oh, that's assured the moment she says she'll marry me!'

Bryony remembered how she had once thought how impossible it would be for her to stay on Petitnue if Dominic ever married. Then the prospect had seemed something distant and too abstract to be considered seriously; now something told her that he was not only considering the idea, but possibly had someone in mind, and the idea stunned her for a moment, partly because she realised she did not want to believe it.

Whether or not she would have questioned him further, she would never know, for at that moment Jules joined them, closely followed by Marie, and pulling a wry face when he looked at his wristwatch. 'Jenny's still sleeping,' he told them. 'I've only just woken up myself. How did you two manage to be so bright and early?' He glanced from one to the other, and it was clear that he sensed something in the air. 'Am I interrupting something?' he asked, half serious, and Dominic shook his head.

'Nothing important,' he said quietly. 'Nothing that won't keep.'

Bryony read her letter through for the third or fourth time and looked up when she heard Jules chuckle. She so seldom received mail that, except for an occasional one from a great-aunt in England, a letter was cause for comment and curiosity.

'If it isn't from your great-aunt Germyn,' Jules said, 'who is it, Bryony? A secret boy-friend?'

Bryony was used to being teased, Jules had always teased her, and she seldom took it to heart, but she answered him with such a vague air of distraction that he looked more curious than ever. An idea had begun to formulate the moment she read the letter for the first time, and the more she thought about it the more convinced she was that she could do it.

'It's from a girl I was at school with.' She folded the single page and put it back in the envelope. 'Her family have moved to Guadeloupe, and she's asked me to go and visit her—they've got a house in St Claude now.'

'It'll do you good.' Jules approved unhesitatingly, although she noticed that Dominic was less quick to pass an opinion. 'You are going?'

'Oh yes, I think so.' It was quite automatic to look at Dominic when she said it, and she wondered why he did not express an opinion too. 'I'll beg a lift over on one of the boats, Dom.'

He took a sip of coffee before he answered. 'Yes, of course, but don't forget to catch the return trip.'

'Oh, not the return trip!' She protested, knowing how little time it would give her when she had in mind to visit Sarah Bryant as well as her old school-friend.

'I don't like the idea of you being stranded if you miss the boat, that's all.' He seemed to catch a certain look in her eye for he raised a hand and there was a smile on his mouth that gave it a slightly lopsided look for a moment. 'I wasn't trying to tell you what to do, *petite*, only thinking ahead.'

It was easy to remember how close she had come to tears yesterday at breakfast, when he had declared himself no longer concerned with her and Tim's activities, so she avoided looking at him and instead looked across at Jules as she suggested an alternative solution.

'I could go over on the *Félicité*—she usually leaves first, doesn't she?—and come back on the *Bonne Chance*. It will give me a bit longer, and I haven't seen Marion for ages.'

'It's not certain the *Bonne Chance* will be ready by Thursday.' Dominic poured himself more coffee, so casual about it all that Bryony began to resent it.

'Then why don't you stay for longer, sweetheart?' The solution came from Jules and she thought Dominic frowned, though she could not be sure. Jules went on, anxious to make her trip as enjoyable as possible and egged on by Jenny, who was nodding agreement, 'If your friend can't put you up, I'm sure old Chaubetain, our agent, would be delighted to have you. His wife likes to have young folks around and they haven't any children.'

'I could ask Marion and find out.' The idea of staying for a day or two appealed to Bryony, for it would make it so much easier for her to seek out Tim's school-teacher, and that at the moment was what she had in mind, regardless of whether or not she was on dangerous ground. 'I'm sure she'll find room for me if she can.'

'The change will do you good,' Jules told her. 'You haven't spent a night away from here since you left school, and that's a year ago.'

'More than a year,' Bryony corrected him hastily. 'I'm nineteen this year, Jules.'

'So you are!' His eyes twinkled good-naturedly. 'Well then, it's time you spread your wings a bit, sweetheart. You're a sensible girl and if you're with your friend's family you'll be O.K.'

'Oh yes, of course!' She agreed hastily, glancing at Dominic as she did so, to see what he made of the idea. 'Is that all right with you, Dom? I can catch up on my jobs when I get back.'

Grey eyes watched her steadily for a moment and she felt a curious little shiver slide along her spine. 'You don't have to ask my permission, *petite*, you are old enough to make up your own mind about spending time with your friend. Of course you can go over on the *Félicité* and come back the same way, there's no problem at all there, but——' He shook his head after a second of consideration and smiled. 'I hope you enjoy your holiday—Jules is right, it's time you spread your wings a little.'

Somehow his words made her feel strangely emotional, as if he had changed her entire life by uttering them, and yet he had said no more than Jules had, in effect. She reached across and laid her own small hand on his, squeezing the hard fingers for a moment.

'I will,' she said. 'Thank you, Dom.'

Tim looked sceptical about the trip having Dominic's

blessing, and his scepticism annoyed Bryony. Somehow lately Tim seemed to have the habit of seeing an ulterior motive in every move Dominic made, and she did not believe it was true, neither did she like to think of him having such an opinion of his half-brother.

'You just won't give Dom credit for being human, will you?' she asked. She sat perched on the divan beside him, waiting for someone to tell her it was time for her to leave. She had Tim's gratitude for her proposed endeavours on his behalf with Sarah Bryant, but he was much too nervously anxious about Dominic finding out. 'He really means it when he says he hopes I enjoy myself, you know, Tim; he was very sweet about it, especially when I'm rather a lot behind with the invoices for the past couple of months.'

'He'd have been a lot less sweet if he'd known you have a letter for Sarah in your handbag,' Tim declared shortly. 'He *doesn't* know, does he, Bry? You haven't let it slip?'

'Of course I haven't!'

His good-looking young face showed a suggestion of a sneer, and Bryony hated it. 'I'll bet he doesn't! He'd never have let you off the leash if he did. You wait until you find yourself a boy-friend and then see how quickly he hauls in the line again!'

Bryony sighed, resigned to his rather petulant ill humour while he was still nursing his broken ribs; no doubt they were painful, and he had never been one to sit around in the house or to take things easy. She got up and walked across to the window, looking out across the garden to where the banana leaves made gigantic scallops against the skyline.

'I'm only going for a few days,' she reminded him,

'and I'm hardly likely to fall in love in a couple of days, am I?'

'Hmm!' He could be as hard-headedly stubborn as Dominic when it came to giving way, and it was at moments like this that she was forcibly reminded that Tim was as closely related to Dominic as he was to her. Sometimes he had a great deal of his French mother in him when he became emotional about something he felt deeply about. 'Is Louis going over with you, or haven't they got the *Chance* patched up yet?'

The fact of the schooner being damaged troubled him almost more than his own injuries, she knew, and smiled at him reassuringly. 'She's ready and I'm going in her with Louis. I know,' she hastened to add when she saw his expression, 'you'll think he's there to keep an eye on me for Dom, but I'd *rather* go with Louis, Tim, and Dom knows I would.' She glanced at her watch, a flutter of excitement stirring in her at the prospect of her trip. 'I'd better go and find Dom, he was putting my things into the jeep and he must be ready for me by now.'

Tim caught her hand as she went to kiss him goodbye, and his eyes searched her face for a second narrowly. 'You won't let me down, will you, Bry? Not even if Dom does get wind of what you mean to do.'

'No—no, of course I won't.'

It was not an easy promise to make when she was very unsure just what she would do if Dominic discovered she was acting as go-between for Tim and his schoolteacher. She straightened up hastily when the door opened and turned to let Dominic know she was ready, blinking uncertainly for a moment when she saw him.

He had changed his clothes since she saw him last, and instead of the casual garb he had worn then he now had on a light grey suit with a cream shirt and a tie, and she felt a sudden fluttering beat to her heart as she stared at him. He smiled, standing in the doorway instead of coming into the room.

'Ready?' he asked, and she nodded automatically.

She could sense Tim's suspicion even without looking at him, and she was much too unsure of her own reactions. It looked as if Dominic meant to accompany her for at least some of the journey, and she could not decide whether or not she welcomed the prospect.

'You look very businesslike, Dom.'

'Good!' He gave Tim a casual wave from the doorway, ignoring the frown that acknowledged it. 'I have some business in Basse-terre.'

'Oh, I see.'

Dominic's grey eyes looked down at her steadily as she passed him in the doorway and she thought they held a hint of a smile, a smile that hovered about his mouth too, without actually appearing. 'I shall be coming with you,' he said quietly. 'You don't mind, do you?'

'Oh no—no, of course I don't!'

He nodded, as if he really had needed her approval before he went, and his fingers slid along her arm as she walked on into the hall. A bright flush warmed her cheeks, she knew, and just before Dominic closed the door behind them, she heard Tim give a derisive snort of laughter.

CHAPTER FOUR

COMING in to Basse-terre never failed to give Bryony a certain thrill of excitement. The trip over from Petitnue was quiet and as always she had enjoyed it, watching the sails billowing overhead and the spindrift fluffing about the bow and curling back into their wake, while the wind tossed her coppery-red hair into tangles she had to do something about before they landed.

Dom stood with her for a while, his grey eyes narrowed against the wind, a commanding figure moving without clumsiness on the deck of the schooner, and lending a steadying hand when her own sea-legs proved less reliable. For some reason she could not yet determine, she had a sense of adventure this trip that she had never experienced before, and she felt convinced it had something to do with the fact that Dominic was with her, though she had made the same trip with him at other times in the past eight years.

Approaching from the sea the shoreline of Basse-terre was dominated by the towering peaks of volcanic La Soufrière and Sans Toucher, wreathed about by circlets of light cloud, and the town itself lying at their feet. Soufrière in particular seemed to brood over the lush countryside and the town, like a benevolent god who could at any time be roused from its benevolence by a quirk of nature.

In the foreground the docks bustled with activity, loading and unloading, a babel of language predominated by French and its lyrical offspring, Creole. The larger freighters as well as schooners like the *Bonne Chance* slid in and out of their berths in a flurry of hurtling lines and calling voices, and Bryony found the non-stop movement and noise quite breathtaking after so long.

Basse-terre itself was a delightful town, a mixture of old and new, with beautiful parks and handsome buildings and an incredibly varied population. It seemed so long since she had been involved in anything more than the tranquil life of Petitnue that Bryony found the sudden bustle incredibly bewildering as well as exciting, so that she willingly left the business of coming ashore in Dominic's capable hands.

He also seemed to take it for granted that she would expect him to drive out with her to St Claude, where her friend lived with her family, though she could perfectly well have gone there herself by taxi. St Claude was at the very foot of La Soufrière, and the spectacular way up to the summit of the mountain started from this exclusive and beautiful little community.

Having delivered her to the gates of the house, Dominic got out and reached in for her *valise*, so that for a moment or two Bryony wondered if he meant to deliver her right to the door. Instead he stood looking down at her for a second or two, while the man waited. Then, quite unexpectedly and with startling suddenness, he put his hands on her shoulders and drew her towards him, pressing his lips in a firm hard kiss over her mouth.

'Enjoy yourself, *petite*, but don't get too much of a taste for city life, hm?'

'I won't.' She laughed and it sounded remarkably unsteady, but her composure was disturbed by the unfamiliar pressure of his mouth on hers. 'I mean, I will enjoy myself, but I don't think I'll get a taste for city life.' She looked around at the big, opulent houses set in gardens of tropical trees and shrubs, and shook her head. 'Although it isn't really city out here, is it? It's a bit like Petitnue.'

•Dominic's attitude puzzled her, for she had never before sensed him so anxious, almost as if he was reluctant to leave her, and she could feel the hardness of his fingers on her arms and the tension in the lean warmth of his body that just touched her while they stood together on the tree-shaded sidewalk.

'But it isn't Petitnue, Bryony, and I hope you won't forget it.' He sought for words of explanation for a second, then shrugged in that indisputably Gallic way he had, and which she now found quite inexplicably touching. 'You're not a little girl, as you're always telling me these days, and I mustn't behave like a guardian or you'll be angry, won't you?'

'Not angry, Dom!' She felt curiously reluctant to see him go now that it came to the point, and she was reminded of those days when she had to leave home to return to school, and how she had always missed his gentle concern for her. Impulsively she tiptoed and reached for his mouth, her lips soft and light, a kiss as breathless as the laugh that followed. 'I'm well able to take care of myself, Dom, and you don't have to sound as if I'm leaving home for good!'

'No.' He let his hands fall and stood back for a moment, his eyes on her face, then he shook his head slowly. 'I simply feel that this is a step in a—a new direction, that's all, *petite*. Your friend is——'

'You've met Marion, don't you remember?'

He was nodding even before she finished reminding him, and she was curious. 'I remember her,' he said, and something in his voice made her even more curious. 'She's a year or two older than you, isn't she, and very —sophisticated?'

'Is she?' She wondered why they hadn't discussed this aspect before they left Petitnue, instead of doing so now while the taxi stood waiting. 'I haven't seen her for a year, but I suppose you could say she was quite sophisticated for her age.'

'Bryony——' He spread his hands in a gesture that suggested resignation, and half-smiled. 'I'll see you on Saturday, huh?'

'You'll come for me?'

Heaven knew what had prompted her to ask him that, but he was looking at her as if it was a matter of course. 'If you'd like me to,' he said. Grey eyes searched slowly over her face and she thought they smiled, a warmth that showed in the dark depth of them without touching his mouth. 'I'll come for you, of course.' Once more he drew her towards him and lightly touched her mouth with his lips. '*Au revoir, petite!*'

Turning from her, he got back into the taxi while she stood watching him, waving a hand to her as he gave the driver instructions in his own tongue, and Bryony was left wondering at the curious sense of loss she felt suddenly. Bringing herself back to earth, she turned and looked at the house as she walked along a wide, tree-shaded driveway.

Tucked away among a riot of hibiscus and frangipani, plumbago and thunbergia, it was virtually half buried in a chaos of colour and scent, and it reminded her once more of Petitnue. The style was similar to the

Laminaire home, but it was newer and, to Bryony's eye,
rather less attractive than the old plantation house.

A balcony ran the width of the house, supported by
slim columns that formed a cool shaded cloister below,
where shuttered windows stood wide, and an arched
doorway, similarly ajar, seemed to suggest a welcome,
although there was no one about to meet her yet. Venturing under the overhanging gallery, she had a hand
already raised to knock on the open door when a young
man appeared in the hall beyond and she hastily lowered her hand.

He was about twenty-three or four, she guessed, and
enough like Marion, her friend, to make a relationship
almost inevitable, and he was smiling with the same
self-confident air that Bryony had always envied at
school. He had changed direction as soon as he saw
her, and he took her bag from her without hesitation,
drawing her inside the house while he shook her hand.

'Hello, you must be Bryony! I can't give you another
name, I'm afraid, because I don't think I've ever heard
it.'

She went with him across a wide airy hall where an
electric fan in the ceiling kept the air constantly moving
and deliciously cool. 'I'm Bryony Charn.'

'And I'm Edward Fuller, Marion's brother.'

Enlightened at last, Bryony smiled. She had been
under the impression that Edward Fuller was still in
England attending university, but obviously things had
changed and Marion had ommitted to mention it. 'I
hope it isn't inconvenient my coming now, Mr Fuller. I
mean if there's a problem about room——'

'The problem will be if you go on calling me Mr
Fuller.' He set down her bag at the foot of the stairs,

presumably to await someone else's attention, and turned to smile at her. 'I'm Ned to everybody I like, and I'm certain I'm going to like you, Bryony.' He had rather nice brown eyes and he was watching her with a suggestion of laughter in them. 'You just missed Marion and Pop; they went to meet you, but you must have passed them on the road somewhere between here and the docks.'

'Oh dear!' So far she had seen no one else about, and she was uncertain just what she ought to do about Marion and her father. 'Should we—I mean should I——'

'Walk the four miles back down into Basse-terre? Oh, I don't think so, do you? I've promised to hold the fort, and that includes entertaining our guest when she arrives.' He led the way into a big, cool room that looked as if it had been transferred complete from an English country house. 'Sit down, won't you?'

He indicated a large and slightly shabby settee just behind her, and she realised with what intent when he sat down beside her. 'I think we docked rather earlier than I told Marion,' she explained, made vaguely uneasy by the frankly admiring brown eyes watching her. 'We had the advantage of the wind, and the *Bonne Chance* always makes the best time.'

'A schooner?' He looked interested. 'Oh, but of course, the Laminaires still use them, don't they?' A short laugh explained his interest. 'I'm supposed to be going into shipping, so I'm swotting up on the various people who trade in and out of the port. You're one of the Laminaires, aren't you?'

'Not exactly, but Dom—Dominic Laminaire, is my guardian. He's the only real Laminaire left now.'

For some reason she found hard to fathom at the moment, she had named Dominic as her guardian rather than her stepbrother. For one thing because it always required an effort to remember the tenuous link that related her to Dominic, for she could never really see him as a relation, even by marriage.

Edward Fuller's interest was quite genuine, she thought, and he smiled enquiringly at her. 'Aren't there two more brothers?'

'Half-brothers,' Bryony corrected him with a smile. 'My father married Dom's mother after she was widowed, and then Jules and Tim were born. When she died he married my mother, so I'm not really related to Dom at all, and Jules and Tim are only half-brothers to him. They're not Laminaires.'

'Complicated!' That self-confident smile stirred curious reactions in her, and she could not yet decide for certain whether or not she liked Edward Fuller. 'So—Dominic?—is the last of the Laminaires? Pity really, they're a very old family in the islands, aren't they?'

'About three hundred years.'

'And now they're dying out.'

'Only if Dom doesn't marry!' Something about that smile of Edward Fuller's brought a bright flush of colour to her cheeks, and she was almost unconscious of sounding defensive. 'He's a young man and he could marry and——' She felt a curious reticence about suggesting that Dominic could be followed by sons of his own, and yet she was sure it was going to happen, especially so since that rather disturbing conversation she had had with him a few days ago. 'I can't se Petitnue ever being without a Laminaire.'

'So Marion might get her way after all, then?' He laughed when she stared at him uncomprehendingly, and shook his head. 'My sister harbours visions of his marrying you,' he explained a little more diffidently, and Bryony felt the colour in her face as she hastily avoided looking at him.

She had never imagined Marion thinking along such lines and the idea of her not only doing so, but making the fact known to her brother made her flush with embarrassment. 'I remember introducing him to Marion last year when Dom fetched me home, when I left school, but I didn't know she knew him apart from that.'

Edward smiled wryly, as if he might have said more than he ought, and she could not help feeling that he was relieved when they heard the sound of a car stopping, followed by voices coming closer and footsteps in the hall. 'And talking of angels,' he said, getting up from his seat beside her, 'I think Pop and Marion are here.'

'Bryony!' The familiar tall thin figure of her schoolfriend seemed to have grown taller in the past year, and she was a little less thin and more shapely, but the biggest change Bryony thought was in her manner. She held out her hands and eyed Bryony critically for a second with the priviledged frankness of long acquaintance. 'You haven't got any taller, have you? And you still wear your hair long!'

After so long Bryony found her rather overwhelming, and some indefinable something in the other girl's manner did not suggest quite the warmth she expected, though she was probably being too sensitive. A hand to

her coppery-red hair, she smiled. 'I like it long best, it seems to suit me better.'

Marion swung her own short brown hair about her lively face and laughed. 'Oh, I shed mine with my school blouse and skirt. Do you like it?' Without waiting for approval, she took Bryony by the arm and turned to introduce her father, a tall grey-haired man who seemed overwhelmed by his daughter's more commanding character. Introductions over, she sat herself down beside Bryony on the settee, her brown eyes eager and curious. 'Did Dominic bring you over?'

Bryony once more felt a flutter of embarrassment when she remembered what Edward Fuller had said about his sister's opinions, and she hastily stifled it with a smile and a nod. 'He was coming over on business anyway, and gave me a lift in his taxi; although I could quite easily have found my own way here.'

'Still taking care of you?' Mischief gleamed in Marion's brown eyes and Bryony hastily avoided them. 'Don't you love it, Bryony? I would!'

Bryony felt strangely out of her depth with this new and very unfamiliar Marion. There was a maturity about her that had, she supposed, developed naturally from the bold self-confidence she remembered from their schooldays, and had so admired. Marion was just over a year older, it was true, but she seemed to have become a definite woman since their last meeting, so that Bryony was not at all sure that she knew this bright, self-assured creature beside her.

'Yes, I suppose I do.' She made the admission cautiously in the circumstances. She would never admit to anyone outside the family that she did not always appreciate Dominic's attitude, but she felt that some-

how Marion suspected it and did not understand it.
'Dom's always taken his role as my guardian very
seriously, you know; I suppose he just hasn't grown out
of it.'

'And you surely don't want him to, do you? I can't
imagine why anyone would object to having a sexy male
like Dominic Laminaire running around after her—I
know I wouldn't!' Apparently heedless of any embarrassment she was causing, she glanced at her wristwatch and then at her father. 'Are you using the car
after lunch, Pop? I thought I might take Bryony for a
run somewhere.'

It was only then that Bryony remembered that she
had a letter to deliver for Tim, and the idea of a ride
suited her. Seeing Mr Fuller relinquish possession of
his car with a shrug of resignation and a wry smile, she
accepted readily.

'That will be lovely; I have a message to deliver for
Tim, if we *are* going out. I don't know where the street
is, but you probably do.' She took out Tim's letter to
Sarah Bryant and showed her the address, and Marion's
fine brows arched curiously.

'A *billet-doux*?' she laughed, and would have taken
the envelope from her if Bryony had not slipped it back
into her bag. 'Don't tell me Tim's carrying on a secret
love affair!'

To Bryony, remembering what a serious view
Dominic took of the affair and what strong feelings it
had aroused between the two men, it was not possible
to treat it as lightheartedly as her friend did, but she
hesitated to confide in her. She no longer felt so close to
Marion as she had expected to, although she still liked
her, and she found it difficult to know how to reply.

'Tim was hurt in that storm we had the other night.' She acknowledged a murmur of sympathy with a nod, and went on, 'He was going to see her—Miss Bryant, yesterday, and by now she must be wondering what's happened to him. I—we thought it might set her mind at rest if I brought her a letter from Tim.'

'All very secret,' Marion said, and her brown eyes were bright with curiosity. 'Couldn't one of you have phoned her?'

'No, not really, not without—everyone knowing.' Bryony held her hands on her lap and looked down at them intently, realising with dismay just how underhand she felt suddenly. 'It's—well, it's a bit awkward really. You see, Sarah Bryant is about thirty-five and Tim's only twenty, and there's been some bad feeling between Dominic and Tim about it.'

'Ah, I see, and if Dominic knew you were carrying a letter to her——' Marion made a sign like a bomb exploding and pulled a face. 'He'd be furious and probably explode!'

'He'd be hurt.' It was an admission Bryony hated to make, and Marion was looking at her with a curiously worldly look in her eyes, disregarding her father's signals that she should leave the matter.

'I see!' She held out a hand and smiled at Bryony's look of bewilderment. 'Well, to ease your conscience, Bry, I'll take it to the lady if you like, then you won't feel quite so conscience-stricken about deceiving Dominic, will you?' She snapped her fingers together, and after a moment Bryony obeyed the signal and handed her the envelope that Tim had entrusted to her care. Turning it over in her hand, Marion smiled at her quizzically. 'I get the feeling that that's what bothers you most, isn't it? You really don't like going behind his back, even for your favourite brother!'

'Not really, but I didn't look at it quite like that in the first place.'

'But now your conscience is bothering you because you know he wouldn't like you playing cupid behind his back!' It was so near the truth that Bryony found it discomfiting, and Marion laughed good-naturedly. 'You always did have a thing about doing something Dominic wouldn't like,' she told her, and Bryony made no attempt to deny it.

It was a relief to know that Tim's letter had been delivered, although Bryony found it rather frustrating that Marion refused to say another word about it, even about what kind of a reception it got from its recipient. The less she knew, Marion told her, the less involved she need feel. Supposing it to be true, Bryony was grateful, but it did not completely banish a niggling sense of unrest she felt at having deceived Dominic.

After delivering the letter, Marion drove them along the old road to Pointe-à-Pitre and, although the scenery was little short of spectacular, it soon became apparent that the main object of the drive was to indulge in conversation without the distraction of Edward. Conversation that turned out to be rather more discomfitingly personal than Bryony anticipated.

For a time talk was concentrated on the countryside around them, while Marion pointed out different aspects of the route to her. Acres of sugar cane with its silvery plumes alternating with the more familiar bananas with their ragged leaves fanned against the blue sky, and countless streams fed by falls that started in the mountains, making the whole lush prospect possible. And beside the more practical vegetation, the vivid exotic colours of hibiscus growing in such profusion and with such abandonment that the whole setting looked too good to be true.

'How long can you stay?'

Snatched from her appreciation of nature at her most flamboyant, Bryony was surprised to realise that this was the first time the question of how long she should stay had been raised. 'Until Saturday, if that's all right, Marion. The *Bonne Chance* will be over again then and I'll go back in her.'

'With Dominic?'

Bryony cast a hasty glance at the dark lively face of the girl beside her. 'Yes—at least, he said he'd be coming for me.'

'Naturally!' Maybe she should not have put it exactly like that, for the look that Marion gave her was loaded with meaning. 'I was hoping it was going to be longer, but I suppose Dominic doesn't like the idea of you being away for too long, especially if he knows Ned is home.'

'He doesn't, you didn't tell me!' It was difficult to simply laugh off the implication, though she tried, watching the riotous colours of the hibiscus as she spoke, and inevitably reminded of the garden at Petitnue. 'It really doesn't matter if he did know, Marion, you've got quite the wrong idea about—about Dom and me, you know.'

'Have I?' There was a ghost of a smile on her rather full mouth whose meaning was unmistakable. Marion had always shown an interest in the somewhat complicated menage that existed on Petitnue, but so far as Bryony could remember, she had never before been so embarrassingly frank as she was now. 'Have I really, Bry?'

Bryony wished she could not so easily remember the kisses that Dominic had pressed on her mouth before he left her, and it was hard to think of an answer when she recalled so vividly the warm touch of his mouth and the hands that had held her close to him for a few seconds. She shook her head, trying to dismiss the sensations that remembering aroused.

'Dom's my stepbrother, Marion!'

Never before had she sought so firmly to establish it, but she knew it made little difference to what Marion had in mind. She was smiling in that discomfitingly knowing way she had. 'You've never gone to much trouble to establish the fact before,' she reminded her, 'and it isn't really important, you know. Your father just happened to marry his mother, long before you were born, and it doesn't in any way bar him from—having ideas about you!'

'Well, you're wrong, Marion, if you think there's anything—anything at all like that!'

'Because he's nearly sixteen years older than you are?' Getting no answer, Marion chuckled quietly to herself and shook her head. 'Oh, don't try and kid me, my girl, I've seen the way you blush whenever his name comes up, and I firmly believe your Dom doesn't believe in practising what he preaches as far as age is concerned—not in this instance anyway!'

Too stunned for a moment by the matter-of-fact way it was all being spelled out to her, Bryony shook her head. The situation that Marion envisaged was too disturbing to be contemplated sensibly, and she did not want to go on talking about it. 'Marion, I wish you wouldn't keep on about it! As you say, Dom is sixteen years older than I am, and he's my guardian, or he was until recently!'

'And he wouldn't be the first man to fall for the girl he's been guardian to,' Marion insisted firmly. 'He might decide that fifteen years is too big a gap between Tim and his lady-friend, but he doesn't have the same reservations about himself!'

'Marion, you can't talk like that when you've never seen Dom, except once!'

'Twice,' Marion corrected her smartly. 'He brought you back one term, I remember, and you looked so woebegone when he left that I swear you were—that way about him even then, when you were only sixteen. I saw the way he greeted you when you left that last term, and the way he looked at you. Oh, for heaven's sake, Bry, you surely felt the way it was, didn't you?'

'No, I didn't!'

Her voice was short and breathless and she sat with her hands in her lap, tightly rolled together, trying to contemplate something that she was not sure she could cope with at the moment. And it seemed almost as if Marion realised how she felt, for she turned her head for a second, then laughed shortly and pulled a face.

'I'm sorry, Bry, I didn't mean to embarrass you. I didn't realise it would come as such a shock to you. I—well, I assumed you knew and just—chose not to recognise it.'

Reluctant to appear so naïve as to arouse sympathy, Bryony made an effort to counter the impression.

Shaking back her hair, she propped an elbow on the car door and rested her chin on her hand, pulling a wry face. 'I must appear as a real country bumpkin to you, don't I, Marion?'

'No, you do not!' The charge was firmly denied, and Bryony sensed some of the old familiar warmth give a boost to her morale as the brown eyes studied her briefly and seriously. 'But you're pretty enough to get under Ned's skin, and I think *he's* going to wish you were staying longer too!'

In a way it was something of a relief the following day when Edward Fuller decided to come with them on a trip to the summit of La Soufrière. At least in the company of her brother Marion would surely keep off the subject of herself and Dominic.

Edward was very obviously smitten and made no effort to disguise the fact, but he had the same forceful and uninhibited manner that his sister did, and at times Bryony found him rather overwhelming. He wasn't unattractive, and yet she felt reluctant to encourage him, without being quite sure of her reasons.

Marion insisted on driving because, she said, she was a much better driver than Edward, and she knew the terrain slightly better. He sat in the seat behind Bryony, leaning forward to rest his arms along the back of her seat, so that she was kept constantly aware of him, and each time he spoke his breath stirred the hair at the nape of her neck, fluttering over her skin with a disturbingly shivery sensation that was not unpleasant.

The way to the summit was narrow though negotiable, and after a while the presence of Edward behind her faded to the back of her mind in the excitement of the trip. They had to brake suddenly when a small, sinuous shape scuttled swiftly across the road and a mongoose slid away into the undergrowth, and at one point the glittering, tumbling mass of a waterfall caught Bryony's eye unexpectedly and made her gasp at the illusion it created.

She had wondered at the need to start so early in the day, but seeing the sun catch the surface of the rushing cataract of water was answer enough, for only at this time of the day could the full breathtaking beauty of it be appreciated.

The need for mackintoshes too had puzzled her until they were obliged to leave the car and continue on foot through the unbelievable world of the rain forest. Huge trees and gigantic ferns thrived in a cool wet world without sun, so quiet that the silence was uncanny, broken only by the never-ceasing splash of the falls. Falls that began at the summit and fell with increasing speed and volume down the whole height of the mountain and, seen in the light of the morning sun, almost too dazzling to watch, pouring like molten gold from a gigantic crucible.

It was only when she realised how she was wishing that Dominic could be there to share the breathtaking wonder of it with her that she eventually turned away. Perhaps he had never seen this stunning spectacle, or perhaps he had not thought to bring her to see it, but suddenly she wanted to tell him about it, to bring him into the enchanted world she found herself in.

Marion took the lead on the way back, and it was when his sister had put some distance between her and Bryony that Edward came up beside her and slid an

arm around her waist, ostensibly with the idea of helping her negotiate the descent. Taken unawares, she
instinctively caught her breath when she felt herself
pulled close against the firmness of a masculine body,
and she looked up into Edward Fuller's smiling face
for a moment without speaking.

'I thought a hand might be welcome,' he said,
almost as if he challenged her to object.

'Thank you.'

'Ned.' She looked at him curiously and he laughed,
his brown eyes still showing that hint of challenge. 'You
always carefully avoid using my name,' he told her,
'and I can't believe it's because you're shy; not when
you have three brothers.'

'Only two!' She made the correction swiftly and
without stopping to think, so that Edward flicked a
brow in question. Sensing his curiosity, she went on
hastily and a little breathlessly, laughing to dispel any
suggestion of seriousness, 'I never count Dom as a
brother, probably because I've always thought of him
in the role of guardian.'

'Oh, I see!' Something about his smile made her
uneasy, so that she looked away again, walking within
the circle of his arm without feeling really happy about
it. 'I thought there might be another reason.'

It was all too clear that he referred to Marion's
speculation regarding her relationship with Dominic,
and she wished it was possible to deny the existence of
such a relationship without making it sound too important. But whatever he believed, it was evident that
he was not going to let it deter him from following his
own interests, for the arm about her tightened, and
she was turned to face him suddenly, looking up into a

face that was half-smiling and damp with the same soft cool rain that moistened her upturned mouth.

It was instinct, she supposed, that made her close her eyes when he bent his head, and the same instinct that made her responsive in the first instance to the touch of his lips on hers. It was not the same firm hardness of Dominic's kisses, but something more basic and insistent, that made her curl her hands against the wet raincoat he wore and, after a second or two, try to break away from him, by pushing hard with both hands against his chest.

It was a second or two before she ventured to look at him, and when she did she saw that faint smile still lingering in his eyes, and giving to his mouth a suggestion of scorn that made her look hastily away again.

'Haven't you been kissed before, Bryony?'

'Yes, of course I have, I——' The need to counter the challenge was irresistible, and yet she did not want him to attribute the wrong cause to her breaking away from him. 'It just doesn't seem like the right time and place, Ned. We——'

'Came to see the sights?' He laughed shortly, then shook his head, holding her arms again for a moment while he looked into her face and the wide uncertain blueness of her eyes. 'Is it because you think your— guardian might object, Bryony?'

She felt the bright warm flush that coloured her cheeks and shook herself free of his hands once more as she turned to follow Marion through the tangle of trees and ferns. 'Dom has no say in what I say or do! Whether you and Marion believe it or not, the only relationship that exists between me and Dom is that of——'

'Brother and sister?' Edward suggested with a hint of malice, once more taking her up before she could finish a sentence. 'But you went to great pains just now to point out that you never think of him as your brother!'

'He's my *step*brother!'

She felt almost out of her depth suddenly, and struggled not only with Edward's determined contrariness, but with her own emotional confusion as well. Then, it seemed, he suddenly regretted having changed the mood of the moment, for he came alongside her again and put an arm around her waist. Hugging her close for a moment, he smiled down at her flushed, damp face.

'I don't want to fight with you, Bryony; I'm sorry.'

It wasn't quite so easy for Bryony to throw off the reaction he had aroused in her; he had come too close to matters that were, to her, too personal to be discussed with strangers, and she merely smiled and shook her head without saying anything.

'You forgive me?'

It was impossible not to, of course, and she nodded. 'Yes, of course, Ned.'

'Good! Then if you're really heart-free, you'd better get used to being kissed, hadn't you?'

He experimented by planting a kiss on her cheek and she looked up at him, shaking her head and smiling. 'Ned, you're incorrigible!' Apparently encouraged, he kissed her again, laughing as they made their way through the rain forest down towards the warmth and sunshine again, and Bryony mused on the fact that there was little time for him to pursue his promise, for tomorrow Dominic would be coming for her.

CHAPTER FIVE

BRYONY had enjoyed herself on the whole, but she still felt a vague sense of dissatisfaction that she could not quite explain. The visit had seemed like an excellent opportunity to talk about old times; gossip about people they had both known, with Marion, but somehow most of the talk had concerned herself and Dominic, and it made her uneasy.

It hadn't been as she envisaged it at all, and she mused on the fact while she sat with Marion and her family, drinking coffee and waiting for Dominic to come for her. Marion's intention had been to drive her down to the dock, but remembering the confusion of her own arrival Bryony had preferred to wait, in case he too arrived early and missed them.

Edward being there had made quite a lot of difference, of course, and thwarted to some extent her anticipated talks about old times with Marion, but she had enjoyed his company for the most part and it was impossible to remain unmoved by his obvious admiration. He had taken her out last night, dining and dancing until very late, and then driven her back along the moonlit road, leaving his intentions in little doubt.

It was very late when they finally arrived back and Edward had gone to bed with a slightly sulky air, so that Bryony suspected he was not accustomed to being denied his own way. He had made it quite plain this morning, too, that he would prefer her to stay longer, convinced no doubt that he could bring her round to his way of thinking, given more time. He was un-disguisedly irritated by his sister's knowing smiles when Bryony shook her head, well aware of the reason for them.

Not that the idea had not occurred to Bryony her-self, for she was flattered and pleased with Edward's open admiration for her, even though she found it rather more than she could cope with at times. But as she pointed out to him when he suggested she stay on, she had a part to play, however small, in the running of the family business. The fact that her contribution was so insignificant that it could easily have been done by someone else was irrelevant, she felt.

'You're a working girl?'

Something about the way he said it made her in-stinctively lift her chin when she looked at him. 'Why not?' she asked. 'I'm not exactly indispensible, but I do have my own little job, and if I'm not there to do it someone else has to.'

'So you're not a lady of leisure after all, eh?' He was looking at her as if he saw her in a different light sud-denly, and she could not decide whether or not he ap-proved, so that she laughed as she sought the answer.

'Do I go down in your estimation if I'm not, Ned?'

'Not in the least!'

His brown eyes scanned her small face in a swift and curious survey that seemed to suggest he was con-sidering the fact of whether or not she was a willing contributor, or if the task was one she was expected to do whether or not she liked it.

'Are you a volunteer, Bryony, or a conscript?'

'A volunteer, of course! I shouldn't be doing it otherwise, Dom doesn't expect it of me!'

His brown eyes glowed, as if she had risen in his estimation, not diminished. 'So you're bright as well as beautiful!'

'I'm useful!' She accepted the compliment with a slightly uncertain laugh. 'I happen to be good at figures and Dom lets me make myself useful in various ways, though nothing very complicated. I quite like the idea I have to admit, because it makes me feel sort of—independent.'

'And that's important to you?'

She was not sure that she followed his meaning, so she simply nodded, turning when the others did, when she heard voices in the hall, and there was nothing she could do about the suddenly increased rate of her heartbeat when she recognised Dominic's unmistakable voice, speaking to the Fullers' maid.

In the same moment she sensed Marion's eyes on her and shook her head almost instinctively at the gleam of meaning she saw there. No amount of denial was going to convince Marion that she had hold of the wrong end of the stick.

'Your escort.' Marion got up from her chair as the door opened and Bryony wondered rather vaguely at how easily she assumed the role of hostess in the place of her late mother. Smiling confidently, she met Dominic part way and extended a hand in welcome. '*Bonjour*, Monsieur Laminaire!'

She was fully aware that Dominic spoke English as well as she did herself, so Bryony assumed that she was simply bent on making an impression with her knowledge of French. She would assume that he remembered her, it would never occur to Marion to think otherwise, and her bright brown eyes were warm and friendly as she welcomed him.

'*Bonjour*, Mademoiselle Fuller.

He took Marion's proffered hand and for a moment Bryony wondered if he would convey it to his lips. He could be very gallant when he had a mind to, and so very French. Her own responses to him startled her so much that she said nothing for the moment, leaving it to Marion to introduce her father and her brother.

He was not expecting to see Edward, that much was obvious, though he made an effort to conceal it, and Bryony considered the possibility of his thinking she had deliberately withheld the information from him. He looked incredibly tall, perhaps because he topped Edward by a couple of inches, and he looked very Gallic in contrast to Edward's Englishness.

He was wearing a light fawn suit and a cream shirt that showed up the darkness of his tan, and there was a coolness, she thought, in his grey eyes. There was also a curious air of aloofness about him that she could not account for at the moment, but which made her uneasy. She had expected him to kiss her just the usual light caress on her cheek, but he didn't, and that too puzzled her : instead he inclined his head almost formally when he turned to her at last, and whatever his eyes would have revealed was hidden by the thickness of dark lashes.

His coolness troubled her without her being quite sure why it should, for it could easily be accounted for by some matter of business that had not gone quite according to plan. Nevertheless she laughed a little unsteadily when he eventually gave her his attention.

'You'll have some coffee before you go, Monsieur Laminaire?'

It was so seldom that Mr Fuller took the initiative that Bryony had almost forgotten he was there, but in this instance he had forestalled his daughter in the matter of hospitality, and Marion hastened to make amends.

'Oh yes, please do have coffee with us, won't you?'

She was smiling at him persuasively, but it was clear that Dominic was proof against her persuasion as he shook his head, a shadow of a smile on his mouth softening the refusal. 'Thank you, but no, Miss Fuller, I really haven't much time before we leave. If Bryony has said her goodbyes and she's ready——'

'Oh, I've been ready for ages, Dom!'

It was probably not very tactful to appear so eager, and she realised it when she saw the face that Edward pulled. 'You can't wait to leave us, can you, Bryony?'

'Oh, I didn't say that, Ned, I've enjoyed myself enormously!'

'Yes, of course you have! Ned knows what you mean as well as we do,' Marion interposed swiftly, her eyes on Dominic, and dark and shining with meaning, so that Bryony felt her face warm with colour. 'Naturally you want to go home—who wouldn't?'

Bryony did not see how Dominic could fail to follow so obvious a hint, though he gave no indication of having done so. Edward, on the other hand, had no doubt at all what his sister implied and he was watching Dominic with frankly speculative eyes, as if he was trying to see what it was about this tall, arrogant man that both Bryony and his sister found so attractive.

It was silly, perhaps even conceited in the circumstances, to think that Edward was jealous, but it seemed to Bryony that he had made up his mind to dislike Dominic, and apart from the relationship that Marion suspected existed, there seemed to be no other reason for it.

He was watching Dominic while he spoke, and there was the same hint of challenge in his manner that she had noticed the day before when he mentioned their relationship. 'I've tried to persuade Bryony to stay longer, Mr Laminaire, but she tells me she has certain obligations.'

The grey eyes watched every flutter of expression that crossed her face, but he gave no indication of what he wanted her answer to be. 'Were you going to stay longer, Bryony, if you hadn't the books to do?'

With no idea what to say, Bryony hesitated for a second or two, trying to make up her mind. She wanted to see Tim to let him know about the letter Marion had delivered for her, but more than that she found herself wanting to be where Dominic was, and that was on Petitnue. Only something in his manner made her anxious without her knowing why.

'I—don't you need me?' she laughed, a huskily unsteady sound that reproached him. 'Or am I so easily replaceable that I haven't even been missed?'

She knew what she wanted him to say, just as she knew, even before he spoke that he wasn't going to give her the answer she wanted. The grey eyes gleamed like steel between thick dark lashes and he seemed curiously detached from any sense of her need, so that she waited breathlessly.

'Of course you've been missed, Bryony, Jenny finds it very quiet without you.'

She thought Marion caught her breath and her own feeling was one of sudden resentment as well as hurt. She had angled for an admission that he had missed her too, and been firmly put in her place, and she felt the undeniable need to hit back.

'Then you'll be glad to have me back even if it's only to comfort Jenny, won't you?'

'We'll see you again, won't we, Bryony?'

From her expression it was evident that Marion had put her own interpretation on that obvious snub and she saw it in a different light to Bryony, for that discomfitingly knowing look was in her eyes once more.

'I shall try,' she promised. 'I really have enjoyed myself, Marion.'

'Then come again!' Edward came closer, taking her hand and bringing his voice down an octave so that it was low and suggestive of intimacy. 'I couldn't face not seeing you again, Bryony.'

She was so often impulsive, Dominic had told her so, and she did not even look at him as she followed her own instincts yet again. 'Why don't you both come over to Petitnue for my birthday in a few weeks' time?'

Dominic had never encouraged visitors to the island, though he had never given a reason for it, and she was in no mood to care for his conventions at the moment. He could hardly refuse to let her invite friends for her birthday, but for all that she held her breath, wondering if he would put his foot down.

Marion was obviously in two minds about accepting without the specific encouragement of the man who had the final word, but not so Edward. He was smiling in a way that almost suggested he would relish Dominic's dislike.

'Marvellous!' He took her hand and held it tightly in his. 'I'd love to come, Bryony.' He lifted her hand to his lips and kissed her fingers lightly, his brown eyes dark and glowing. 'I can't imagine anything more romantic than a lovely girl on a small Caribbean island —mmm!'

Marion, she noticed, was watching Dominic, waiting for him to confirm the invitation, and for a moment she resented the gesture, no matter if it was prompted by no more than good manners. 'You don't mind if Marion and Ned come over for my birthday, do you, Dom?' She put her friend's question into words, and Dominic shook his head.

'Of course not.' The grey eyes turned on her once more, and the look in them made her hastily lower her own. 'Why should you expect me to mind?' He gave her little time to answer, but glanced at his wristwatch. 'It's time we were going; I promised Louis we'd be there in plenty of time and we're cutting it a bit fine.'

'Yes; yes, of course.'

'We'll be over for your birthday!' Marion hugged her affectionately. 'It'll be so exciting, Bry, I've always wondered about your beautiful island.'

Casting a swift sideways glance at Dominic, Bryony smiled a little ruefully. 'Dominic's beautiful island,' she corrected her, and Marion shook her head at her.

'Bryony!'

Whether it was done with the intention of giving Edward a few seconds in which to say goodbye, Bryony wasn't sure, but she somehow found herself left for a moment in the room with him while the others walked on out into the hall, and as soon as backs were turned he took her in his arms and kissed her.

It was unexpected, although it should not have been, she realised, and she was not aware that anyone had seen it happen until she stepped back, slightly breathless, and saw Dominic watching from the hall. There was barely time to register a fierce glittering look of anger before he turned quickly with a murmured word to Marion and her father, and went striding off out of the house, leaving her to follow alone.

Stunned for a moment at the naked fury she had seen in his eyes, Bryony stared after him, then hurried out into the hall, pulling her hands from Edward's with a gesture of impatience, and as she passed Marion in the hall her friend touched her arm and smiled encouragingly.

'Don't worry,' she whispered, and Bryony wished it was as easy to do as it sounded.

Bryony leaned back against the rail, glad of the dark glasses she wore to hide the troubled look in her eyes. Dominic had said very little to her since they came aboard, and he stood now, talking with one of the hands, for'ard, while she watched from the stern, her restless gaze flitting between Dominic and Louis's broad, unresponsive back where he stood at the wheel.

The wind stirred her hair, blowing it about her face, warm and soft for all its briskness, and the *Bonne Chance* skimmed through the wine-dark water easily, dipping and turning, her sails taut and casting shadows that constantly changed. Ahead Bryony could see the white beaches of Petitnue with their fringes of green palms, becoming clearer every minute, while behind them the hazy sweep of Guadeloupe slowly merged into the skyline, but Bryony had never before faced a homecoming with such a disturbing sense of unease as she did now.

They skirted the shallows off the beach where she had sat with Tim, and the colour and peace of the gardens looked incredibly close, the roof and the upper windows of the house just visible above the tops of the trees. Around the tip of the island and along the north-west side of the quay; a familiar route that somehow lacked some of its usual sense of peace, and the fact made her respond only vaguely to Louis's hasty glance as he brought the schooner up to her mooring.

It wasn't until he was helping her ashore, a service usually performed by Dominic, that she had the first inkling of what was in store. Louis's strong hands squeezed hers for a second and he looked down at her earnestly after glancing over his shoulder to see where Dominic was.

'He knows, *maîtresse*!' Seeing her look vaguely uncomprehending, he added another swift whisper before he released her hands. 'He knows 'bout that letter for Tim's woman!'

'Oh no!'

Bryony stared after him as he leapt nimbly back on board, and noticed that Dominic was coming ashore— a tall, dark and somehow menacing figure, though it was hard to imagine why she saw him in that light suddenly. The jeep stood near the sheds at the other end of the quay and for a second or two she even toyed with the idea of walking back through the groves to the house instead of driving with him in his present discouraging mood.

It was easier, however, to simply take her place beside him in the jeep, though the seat struck uncomfortably hot through the thin dress she wore and she caught her breath, leaning away from the seat-back. Tim would enlighten her soon enough when she got back to the house, but she wished Dominic would tell her how he felt—it would be a relief.

They were driving along the road between the groves and the sea when she half-turned in her seat suddenly, finding the urge to question him too strong to resist. 'Dom.' She fixed her eyes on the dark implacable face with an anxiety she was barely aware of. 'What's wrong?'

For a few moments she thought he wasn't going to answer her, but then he spoke in a flat, matter-of-fact voice that was little more encouragement than his silence had been. 'You're the matter, Bryony—I don't feel I know you any longer!'

'Oh Dom, no!' He said nothing more and she pleated the hem of her dress in nervous fingers for a while trying to find the right things to say. 'I suppose you think badly of me for taking that letter to Sarah Bryant.'

'It would have been more flattering if you'd confided in me, instead of using a visit to your friend as a cover for acting as Tim's go-between! Or should I say friends?'

'Did Tim tell you about it?'

It was possible, she knew, for Tim had never been very good at hiding anything and basically he had disliked deceiving Dom as much as she did herself. But he was shaking his head to deny it and she scarcely believed it could have been Louis.

Briefly a tight, twisted smile touched his mouth, as if he could follow her train of thought. 'And you know better than to suspect Louis!'

'Then——'

'Would it surprise you to know that Miss Bryant her-self told me?'

Too stunned to say anything for a moment, Bryony clung tightly to the side of the jeep while he swung it round another corner, blinking in bewilderment when he pulled over to the side of the road and braked to a halt, stopping so suddenly that she was thrown for-ward in her seat, then pressed back against it by a strong arm that prevented her from hitting her head on the windscreen.

Behind him the huge fronds of the bananas rustled in the wind, ragged fans of glossy green against the blue sky, casting shadows across his face that gave it a rugged darkness that was almost primitive. Bryony sat curiously expectant as she sat half-facing him, and her heart was thudding hard, catching at her breath so that she could not keep her voice steady.

'You—you've seen Sarah Bryant?'

'Does it surprise you to discover that I have a certain amount of compassion in my make-up, Bryony?' That bitter look was on his mouth once more and he shook his head. 'I confess I don't act on impulse very often, but when I'd finished my business on Thursday, after I'd left you, I thought about how close Tim had come to being lost in that storm, and I thought someone should let her know he was all right. I don't believe for one minute that there's anything serious in the affair, but——' His broad shoulders expressed it all with a shrug, and Bryony felt a curiously warm glow suddenly.

'Oh, I'm glad, Dom!'

'To discover that I'm human enough to think of other people's feelings?'

'You know it wasn't that! I wish I could have told you about the letter, but—oh, you know how it was!'

'You thought I'd react like the bully you so obviously think me, so you decided to play Cupid and not say anything! I'm flattered, *petite*!'

'Dom, stop it, please!' It was not like him to be so bitterly angry over nothing worse than Tim's letter and, even now she knew how much he had resented not being trusted, she sensed no let-up in his anger—there was something else. It was still hard for her to believe he had been so angry when Edward took her in his arms and kissed her, and she watched his face as he kept it turned in stern profile. 'Dom, I—I didn't know Edward was going to be at home.'

'No?' He did not question her picking on that subject, and from his tone it might have been thought he was coolly indifferent, but Bryony knew him better than that, and the different stress on his words told her she was right. 'It was no more than a coincidence that he was there then, huh?'

He sounded very French whenever he was angry or emotional, and he was much more inclined to use his hands as well as a more fluid inflection in his voice. Close beside him on the seat of the jeep she was conscious of the tautness of his body and the violence of whatever passion possessed him at the moment.

'Marion hadn't said anything about him being there.'

'You've met him before?'

He was thinking of that parting kiss, of course. It had given the impression that their relationship was on a much more intimate footing than it was in fact, but she did not quite see how she was going to convey that to Dominic.

'I've never met him before Thursday, although I knew *of* him, of course—he and Marion are very close.'

'And she has plans to see you marry her good-looking brother, is that the scheme?'

His reaction to the idea was quite plain, and she spoke up hastily, though without betraying in which direction Marion's plans did lay. 'Not at all, she—well, she isn't thinking along those lines at all.'

Judging by his present attitude it seemed disturbingly likely that Marion was on the right track, but the thought was too disturbing to be considered seriously, and she preferred to think that it was in his role of guardian that he objected so fiercely to Edward kissing her. With the idea in mind of reassuring herself on that, she ventured to explain.

'You—you seemed very angry back there at Marion's house, I wondered if—well, if it was because you saw Edward kiss me.'

For a moment she looked directly into his eyes, dark and grey, like the sky when it stormed and yet with a certain glowing warmth in their depths that made her heart race suddenly. 'I have no right to object to his kissing you, have I, Bryony?'

His voice was quiet, soft almost, and yet so strangely unfamiliar that she rolled her hands tightly together and caught fast at the soaring response of her senses that threatened to get out of control. It was so quiet on the deserted road, and only the rustling sound of the wind in the trees and the shushing of the sea close by competed with the heavy thudding beat of her heart as she tried hazily to find words to answer him.

'I—I suppose not.'

'Hmm.' The noncommittal sound told her nothing

of what he was feeling, but he made no move yet to re-start the jeep and she wondered how deeply he meant to probe into Edward's attitude towards her.

'It—that kiss, it really didn't mean anything at all, Dom. Not to me.'

'But to him perhaps, huh?'

'I don't know. I—I scarcely know Ned, so it's not very likely he's serious.'

'That wasn't the impression I got!'

Noting the sudden harshness in his voice again, she glanced at him from the corner of her eye, and saw a ghost of that earlier passionate fury that had sent him striding out of the Fuller house. She told herself that she could have been angry too, at his too close interest in her affairs, but she wasn't, and it puzzled her briefly.

'I think that Edward Fuller is very likely going to fall in love with you if he sees you too often,' Dominic said. 'You do realise that, don't you?'

It was a possibility, Bryony was bound to admit, but not something she wanted to think about yet, and she shook her head, as if by refusing to recognise it, it wouldn't happen. 'I don't want him to, Dom, I don't want anyone to—at the moment.'

'No one at all?'

He asked the question softly, and when she didn't answer, a brief smile touched his mouth and shone for a moment in his eyes. Then he turned and switched on the engine, bringing a moment's contact with the warmth of his body when he reached out, but he did not immediately drive off. Instead he sat looking at her for a moment, his grey eyes shadowed by their lashes.

'It is good to have you home, *petite*; and now I must take you back or someone will think I am taking awful

vengeance on you for deceiving me!' Laughing as if
the idea amused him, he set the jeep in motion and
headed for home once more. 'I've been made aware
just lately that my family see me as something of a
martinet!'

'Oh no, Dom!' Her fingers tightened about his tanned forearm and he turned his head briefly to smile
at her. 'It isn't true, and you must know it isn't!'

'No?' the inflection in his voice and the sound of
his laughter teased her senses. 'I hope not, *ma chère*,
I do hope not.'

Tim was watching her curiously, Bryony was well
aware, although she did not yet give him the satisfaction
of knowing it, but concentrated on reading her letter.
His ribs were mending fast, and he was chafing at the
delay in being allowed to travel across to Basse-terre,
so that he was ripe for mischief.

He was still faintly puzzled by Dominic's lack of opposition to the plan, and sometimes Bryony suspected
that he actually thrived on opposition, especially when
it came from Dominic. He had noted her frown and it
made him curious, curious enough to crane his neck
to try and read the handwriting on the envelope beside
her plate.

It was the second letter she had received in little
more than a week, and that was in itself cause for
curiosity, but this present one was giving her a lot less
pleasure than Marion's had, although it too contained
what could be construed as an invitation. It could, if
she took its contents seriously, as she was obviously
intended to do, cause a great deal of upheaval.

Able to recognise the writing at last, Tim pursed his

lips curiously. 'What's your Aunt Germyn got to say that doesn't suit you?' he asked with a frankness that earned him Jules disapproval.

'None of your business,' Jules informed him, shaking his head reprovingly. 'And pass the coffee down this way, will you?'

'I just thought it might be trouble, from the way Bry's frowning.' Tim did not let go easily once he was interested, so that Bryony knew she might as well enlighten him now as later.

Folding the letter into four again, she tapped the edge of the paper against her teeth while she considered for a moment before she said anything. And then it was to Dominic that she spoke, not to Tim. 'Dom——' He looked up, frowning curiously when he saw how preoccupied she was. 'I can't be made to go back to England, can I? I mean, I'm old enough to refuse if I don't want to go, aren't I?'

'As long as it isn't something official——'

'Oh no, it isn't!'

He realised it was important to her, it was clear from the way he looked, and presently he reached over and stroked one long forefinger across the back of her hand. 'Then as far as I know, no one can make you go back, *petite*.' He too looked at the letter she held, mildly enquiring. 'Is there any reason why anyone should try?'

It was in Bryony's mind to give him the letter to read for himself, but her great-aunt had been rather too explicit in her reasons and she could not face the prospect of Dominic finding out. Instead she pushed the letter back into its envelope and did her best to convey the general gist of what it contained without going into too much detail.

'Aunt Germyn suggests that I go back to England to live, she—she thinks it would be better if I did.'

'Bry?'

Tim was looking at her more curiously than ever, and she knew that he at least would not want her to go. But it was to Dominic that she gave her attention still, and her eyes were big and anxious as she made her appeal. 'I don't want to go, Dom.'

It was hard to tell exactly how he felt about it, for the grey eyes were hidden, and Bryony watched him, trying to find some hint of reassurance in the rugged dark features. She thought she knew how he would react , but yet she felt a curiously disturbing sense of uncertainty suddenly.

'She doesn't like the set-up here, of course.' He spoke so matter-of-factly that for a moment she simply stared at him and, after a second or two, he looked across at her and smiled. 'Does she know about Jenny being here?'

'Why, yes, of course, I told her when Jules got married.'

From Jules' carefully lowered gaze she knew that he too had no difficulty in following exactly what Aunt Germyn was getting at, and only Tim either did not, or refused, to recognise it. He had an all too familiar defiant look on his face as he looked from Bryony to Jules and to Dominic.

'I don't see what there is to be made of this—set-up, as you call it. Living here with her sister-in-law and her three brothers; where's the wrong in that?'

'No wrong, Tim.' Dominic spoke quietly, as he

mostly did in moments of doubt, but there was something in the way he kept his eyes averted from her that
was not like him, and Bryony found it infinitely disturbing. He ran a forefinger around the rim of his cup,
elbows resting on the table. 'I think Bryony's aunt is
simply trying to point out that not all of us are as
closely related to her as you imply.'

Tim was surely being deliberately obtuse in his
defiance. 'I know Jenny isn't——'

'Or me.' Dominic looked up at last and the grey
eyes held Bryony's steadily for a moment. 'Isn't that
the gist of it, Bryony?'

She nodded, too confused to do anything else. She
supposed she had said too much about Dominic in her
recent letters to Aunt Germyn, mentioned him too
often and in such a way that her great-aunt had read
more into them than she had intended she should. She
was an old lady and she would take a much more
serious view of what a younger woman would probably
have speculated on without worrying about it.

Bryony was nearly nineteen, she reminded her, and
too adult now to be in the care of a man of only thirty-
four, especially such a man as Dominic Laminaire
sounded to be. It had been well enough when Bryony
was still a child, but she was no longer as happy about
the situation now, and especially in view of Bryony's
obvious admiration of the man.

In the circumstances she felt she must recommend
a return home to England, and a stay that was at least
long enough to ensure she was mature enough to see the
pitfalls of such an arrangement. There was no attempt
to disguise the fact that Aunt Germyn visualised her
falling in love with Dominic, and Bryony was not sure

she could deny it with any degree of certainty, even though she had tried so hard and so often lately not to recognise the possibility.

'I don't want to go, Dom.'

She could only repeat her earlier words, praying that Jules or Jenny would intervene; someone who would save her from having to debate the matter with Dominic on her own, for she felt so sure suddenly that he would not give her the unqualified assurance she would once have expected of him.

But no one did, and once more it was he who took up the matter, soft-voiced and not exactly blaming her, but sure she must have given cause for the old lady's anxiety. 'What have you said about the situation here that makes her so suddenly uneasy, Bryony?'

'I don't know—how could I?'

It wasn't the truth and Dominic knew it, shaking his head as he sipped his coffee. 'Something must have put the idea into her head, *petite*, or why should she suddenly have qualms about your position here? Does she suggest that I might—take advantage of my position?' One large and expressive hand conveyed a great deal more than the words, and she felt herself colouring furiously, while Tim's sudden explosion of laughter did nothing to ease the situation.

'Tim!'

She glared at him so furiously that he subsided, looking to Jenny to support him, and shrugging in imitation of Dominic at his most French when her support was not forthcoming. 'Well, you don't have to do as the old lady tells you, do you?' he asked.

Tim was naturally anxious for her not to leave, and Bryony appreciated his anxiety as she looked at Dominic, vaguely uncertain. 'Dom, do you——'

Dominic took another sip from his coffee and shook his head, and there was a hint of smile on his mouth when he looked at her again. 'The final decision to go or stay must be yours, *mignonne*, you must realise that. You are old enough now to make up your own mind about such things—and I quote your own feelings on the subject,' he added with a glint of sardonic humour. 'You must decide whether to go or stay.'

If only he would give away something of his own feelings, it would make her feel so much better, but she watched him for what seemed like an eternity, and the dark face remained impassive. He did not look at her directly again. Spreading her hands in a gesture of helplessness, she appealed to Jules.

'Jules, what should I do? I know Aunt Germyn can't make me go back, but if you all think I should go just to——' She shook her head, realising how close to tears she had come in the few minutes since Tim had queried the contents of her letter. 'Oh, I don't see why I should go, but if Dom doesn't——'

'Speaking for us,' Jules told her, taking Jenny's hand and smiling at her while he spoke, 'we want you to stay, sweetheart; we'd be lost without you.'

Tim, not to be outdone and obviously impatient with Dominic's refusal to persuade her, gave her a broad wink and grinned at her encouragingly. 'You can't leave here, Bry, you'd never survive in the outside world, and Dom knows that as well as anybody. Can you see yourself settling down in—suburban Surbiton, or wherever it is? You'd fade away and die without the sun, you know you would!'

Her eyes were fixed on that dark rugged face, but

still he did not betray by as much as a flicker of an eyelid how he felt, one way or the other, and she felt a sudden aching hurt at his seeming detachment.

'Carried unanimously,' Tim declared, but she shook her head.

'Not quite, Tim.'

There was a wavering unsteadiness in her voice and Jules glanced first at her and then at Dominic, then he gave her a wink, as Tim had done, and he was smiling. 'Oh, I think we can say it's unanimous,' he said confidently.

CHAPTER SIX

FOR the first time since she had issued that spur-of-the-moment invitation to Marion and Edward, Bryony mentioned it to Dominic. The time was getting near and definite plans had to be made one way or the other, but because Dominic had not answered her immediately when she mentioned it, she looked at him with a hint of challenge in her blue eyes.

Whenever she had work to do she borrowed a corner of his office, usually when he was busy elsewhere, and she had thought it a good plan to mention it to him when he came in at the end of the day—although she realised now that it was probably not the best time.

'You haven't changed your mind about letting them come, have you, Dom?'

He was perched on the edge of her desk smoking a cheroot and he swung one leg backwards and forwards while he studied her for a moment through eyes narrowed against the soaring smoke. There was a disturbing steadiness about his gaze that she eyed with suspicion, shifting uneasily to avoid it.

'My dear child, to hear you talk anyone would think I was running some kind of a Devil's Island here! You come and go as you please and so does everyone else, so why should you imply that I forbid you visitors?'

Bryony shrugged, allowing him some reason for exasperation, for he never had restricted their comings and goings. It was simply that she remembered his mood at the moment when she had issued the invitation, and she had the idea that he did not altogether like the young Fullers very much.

'You didn't really expect me to change my mind, did you, Bryony? You know me better than that!'

'I wish I *did* know you!'

The retort was impulsive, as her responses to him so often were, and she fidgeted on her chair when he smiled. Getting up suddenly, she would have brushed past him, but long hard fingers fastened themselves around her wrist and held her, while the grey eyes watched her face, their expression still concealed by dark lashes.

It was so hard, whenever she was near him, not to remember the implications in that disturbing letter of Aunt Germyn's, and she felt as if nothing had been quite the same since the day it arrived. Dominic had guessed easily enough what the gist of it was, and she only wished she knew what his true reaction was to the idea of her going back to England for a time. Her own feelings were in no doubt at all, Petitnue was her home now and she did not want to leave it for any reason at all.

Dominic still needed to look down at her, even though he was seated on the desk and she was standing, and she was much too aware of the virile, almost earthy touch of him where their bodies were in contact. The cotton shirt he wore with close-fitting denims showed signs of a day's wear in the hot sun, stained with green, as if a hand had been carelessly wiped clean against it, and there was a warm, masculine scent about him that touched her senses and made her head swim. Looking down at the arm he held, she wondered vaguely how he could hold her so firmly and not hurt her.

'How long will they be staying?'

The quiet matter-of-factness of the question jolted her back to reality with a suddenness that made her stare at him for a moment without answering. 'I—I don't know; probably just a few hours. Just—long enough.'

'They'll be staying overnight, surely?'

It simply hadn't occurred to her to think about the visit in such detailed terms yet, and she shook her head once more. 'I hadn't really thought about it, Dom, but it would be nice—if you don't mind.'

'Don't you want them to stay over?'

His insistence made her slightly uneasy and she glanced up at his face before she replied, but found nothing there to tell her what he wanted himself. 'Yes, of course I'd like them to stay, but——'

'Does the thought of having Edward Fuller here for any length of time bother you?'

She hastily avoided his eyes once more and shook her head, a tiny frown drawing her brows together for a moment. 'No, of course it doesn't, Dom. We've been into all that—Ned Fuller doesn't matter to me one way or the other. I hardly know the man!'

The strong fingers that curved about her arm had a gentle soothing quality that was more of a caress than a restraint on her movements, and his thumb moved lightly over the pulse spot on her wrist. 'Then you'd better tell Marion that they're welcome to stay for several days if they'd like to. It hardly seems worth making the trip for no more than a few hours. See Marie and she'll organise a couple of spare rooms for them.' A dark brow flicked upward and she met the bright glowing humour in his eyes for a moment. 'I can't have your friends sharing your poor opinion of my hospitality, can I?'

'Dom, I didn't suggest that at all!'

The slow shaking of his head silenced her, and the hand that was holding her wrist released her after a moment to rest at her waist with a warm intimacy that she found infinitely disturbing, and he was laughing at her. His dark face warmed with it, and strong white teeth gleamed in the glowing brown of his features.

'Everything about you shows how surprised you are that I'm making perfectly normal plans to welcome your guests,' he teased. 'Admit it, *petite*!'

Bryony could never get used to the fact that when he teased her, as he was now, he reminded her so strongly of Tim, and each time it happened she was reminded anew of the fact that he was as closely related to Tim as she was herself. Facing the fact of Dominic being related to her in any way was something she was always very unwilling to do, without quite knowing why.

'It was just that—well, I wasn't quite sure how you'd feel about having Ned here.'

'You mean because you hardly know him?'

He was being deliberately difficult, she knew it, and it angered her briefly, so that she looked up at him and stuck out her chin. 'I mean because you were so angry about him kissing me when I left Basse-terre! I thought you might object to having him stay here because you didn't approve of his—his behaviour!'

It was impossible to read what was in his eyes even had she ventured to try, but his voice still had a suggestion of laughter in it. 'He is a very attractive man, young and good-looking, and a very determined one, I imagine. He means to see you again and I've no doubt you'll agree to seeing him, but at least while he is here I can keep an eye on him, huh?'

She really believed he meant just what he said and Bryony was appalled at the idea of him keeping guard on her. Pushing away his hand from her waist, she stepped back, her eyes bright and glowing with indignation.

'Dom, you dare!'

'Huh?' He was still laughing and he reached out his hand again, drawing her back to him and looking down into her eyes with a bright gleaming warmth in his own. 'Don't you like the idea of me making sure you're all right? Safe from the attentions of this—stranger?'

'Oh, you're being unfair and—and maddening! It has nothing to do with you if Ned Fuller kisses me, and you aren't my guardian any more!'

'You wish to dispense with my services, eh?'

'Dom——' She hadn't meant to sound quite so ungrateful or so final, and she fluttered her hands uneasily as she sought for a way to tell him so. 'I didn't mean it like that, you know I didn't.'

It sounded so ineffectual after her anger of a few seconds before, and she was aware suddenly when she looked at him that he was more sober, the laughter had gone, replaced by something infinitely more disturbing. His gaze moved slowly over her flushed face and rested for a moment or two on her parted lips, then he smiled.

'You're very lovely when you're angry, *ma petite*, has Edward Fuller learned that much about you yet?'

Bryony wasn't sure what she was thinking about. She remembered arguing with Edward, about Dominic and her relationship with him, while they made their way back through the rain forest, and she recalled how she had not been persuaded by all Edward's charm after their evening together. Tremblingly uncertain, she was aware of a different mood in the lean dark face so close to her own; the eyes no longer laughing, but deep and unfathomable and breathtaking.

The hand at her waist slid round to her back and tightened its hold, imperceptibly at first, the arm encircling her irresistibly drawing her closer. Another large hand spanned the back of her head with its long fingers twined tightly into her copper-red hair, and the hard, masculine touch of his body seemed to be urging her ever closer until she closed her eyes and let the excitement of it fill her with strange new sensations.

Warm breath fanned her cheek for a second and then her lips, and she felt the light teasing touch of a hard mouth seeking a response from her trembling uncertainty. A whirling chaos of excitement spun around in her head and lifted her to heights she had never dreamed of, but before the thrilling prelude was com-

pleted a sound somewhere snatched back her consciousness, and a voice, vaguely indistinct, said something she
did not hear.

It was instinct that made her bow her head and rest
her forehead on Dom's broad shoulder while she sought
to recover her breath, and she was trembling so much
that she needed the hand she clung to so tightly for
support, if she was not to succumb to the sudden weak-
ness in her legs.

Dominic was looking across at the doorway when she
raised her head, his eyes storm-dark in the brooding
ruggedness of his face, and his voice was much deeper
and more vibrant than she ever remembered it before.
Turning her head, she hastily registered a look of indecision on Jenny's face as she stood just inside the
room, glancing from one to the other, the tip of her
tongue flicking anxiously over her lips.

'What is it, Jenny?'

She shook her head and looked as if she would have
preferred to turn and flee rather than deliver her message. 'I'm—I'm sorry, Dom, I didn't——'

'You timed your entrance perfectly!'

It was impossible to tell whether it was anger or relief
that put such depth into his voice, but Jenny was obviously aware that she had come upon something she felt
she should not have witnessed, and she hesitated before
going on. That dark brooding look of Dominic's could
have given her little encouragement.

'Marie was asking how long before you'll be ready
for dinner. I think she's running a little late, and she
wondered——'

'Tell her she needn't worry!' He got up from the
desk, letting go of Bryony's hand to retrieve the cheroot

he had been smoking from the ashtray beside him. 'I have to bath and change yet, so I'll be another fifteen or twenty minutes before I'm ready.'

'I'll tell her.' Jenny's anxious eyes flicked briefly in Bryony's direction, then hastily back to Dominic. 'I'm sorry, Dom, I should have knocked.'

'Don't be sorry—you probably stopped me from doing something we'd both have been sorry for!' He sounded remarkably cool, and yet Bryony noticed that he did not once look at her as he walked across the room to where Jenny still hovered in the doorway. Smiling at her, he reached out and touched her cheek lightly with a finger-tip. 'Make it ten minutes, *ma chère*, it won't take me very long to shower.'

He was gone, with Bryony's eyes following his lean arrogance out of the room and across the hall before she ventured a glance at Jenny. It was the first time she ever remembered feeling ill at ease with her sister-in-law, and she felt strangely resentful of Dominic's ability to recover so quickly. Tidying things on her desk gave her hands something to do, and she couldn't decide whether or not she was pleased that Jenny still lingered just inside the room.

'Shall I wait for you, Bryony? Or are you changing too?'

It was almost a relief to be addressed directly, and she turned quickly, spreading her hands as she looked down at the blue cotton dress she was wearing. 'Should I, do you think?' It was then that she noticed a crushed leaf stain left on her dress by close contact with Dominic's shirt, obviously, and she put a hand self-consciously to her breast. 'I'd better,' she added breathlessly, and found her legs to be horribly unsteady when she walked across the room.

Jenny's uncertainty did not surprise her, for her sister-in-law was never anxious to become involved in things she thought of as strictly family, even though Jules was for ever urging her to make her presence felt in the same uninhibited way that the rest of them did. She was fond of Bryony and she did not need to be very astute to spot that Bryony had been just as affected, or more so, by the incident she had interrupted, as Dominic was; yet she hesitated to say anything.

It was in an effort to break the uneasy silence that Bryony laughed, though it was a small unsteady sound that was accompanied by the defensive tossing back of her hair from her face. 'If Dom can make it in ten minutes, so can I,' she said. 'What's Marie giving us, Jenny, do you know?'

'I asked for stuffed crab with rice again—I hope nobody minds.'

'I don't see why they should!'

'Sometimes I'm not sure what I ought to ask Marie to do, I'm still not very good at organising menus for a French household even after three years.'

Bryony was only giving half her attention to what was being said and she smiled rather vaguely to dismiss Jenny's doubts about her organising abilities. 'Dom's the only one of us who's really French, the rest of us are——' She shrugged carelessly, finding the matter unimportant at the moment. 'Anyway, no one has any complaints as far as I know.'

'Certainly no one's complained to me.'

'Then I shouldn't worry about it.'

They walked together as far as the foot of the stairs,

and it was clear that Jenny had it in mind to say something, something that Bryony would rather she didn't say. Much as she hoped to avoid it, however, she was already on the first step when Jenny found her voice again, and she turned slowly back to her, and very unwillingly, she admitted.

'Bryony—I just don't know what to say.' She used her hands in a way she must surely have learned from Jules, and her eyes were uncertain as she looked at her. 'I had no idea—I mean, if I'd realised that——' She shrugged again, using her hands to try to convey her apology. 'I could have knocked or—or something, but I didn't expect——'

'Neither did I!' Bryony's voice was light but not quite steady and it betrayed something of the way she was feeling, so that it was not unexpected when Jenny closed her gentle fingers over her hand where it held tightly to the newel post at the bottom of the stairs. 'I hope you don't think that sort of thing goes on all the time in the office,' she said, still trying to make a joke of it. 'It's—it's the first time, Jenny.'

'I didn't know, I wondered if——'

'Don't wonder any longer!' Bryony knew her voice sounded just a little too bright and forced, but there was nothing she could do about it. 'And you won't have to bother about interrupting anything like that again, Jenny, not if I know Dom!'

'And you do, better than any of us, I think.'

Jenny's quiet voice carried confidence, and Bryony looked at her for a moment, her blue eyes evasive and uncertain. 'Do I?' she asked, and gave a little laugh. 'I didn't realise I did—in fact I can't believe it, or I'd have known what was going to happen when——' She shook her head hastily, and Jenny's fingers squeezed hers reassuringly.

'Poor Bryony!' Her gentleness seemed to suggest that she saw herself dealing with a hurt child, and Bryony was not happy about that, but she refrained from saying so, for Jenny, as always meant well. 'Dom can be pretty—well, he's pretty devastating, isn't he?'

It was something in her voice that made Bryony look up and search for something in that gauntly pretty face; something different and unexpected. 'You find him so?'

'Of course, don't you?'

Bryony nodded, trying to decide what was in those hastily concealed eyes. Jenny had always held Dominic in awe, ever since Jules brought her there as his bride, three years ago, but it had never entered Bryony's head that she would ever have eyes for anyone else. Hearing her admit to finding Dominic devastatingly attractive jolted her into a new awareness of her sister-in-law, and she found it vaguely disturbing.

'I didn't realise you—recognised the existence of any other man but Jules,' she explained. 'It just hadn't occurred to me that you—well, found Dom attractive.'

Jenny's skin was still fair even after three years in the Caribbean sun and it flushed a bright pink as she stood looking at her hands rather than at Bryony. 'Don't get me wrong, Bryony. I love Jules more than anything in the world, and there's nothing like that about—well, don't think I nurse an unrequited passion for Dom, or anything like that. But would it shock you to learn that I almost changed my mind about marrying Jules when I realised it would mean living on this island with Dom in command?'

Bryony wasn't sure what to say. It was easy enough

to realise how Jenny felt when she saw her prospective brother-in-law for the first time, but just the same she had not seen Jenny as easy to impress and she wondered if she really knew her as well as she had thought she did. Not that she doubted Jenny's loyalty to Jules for a moment, but it was disturbing to think of her feeling anything more than the awe she always showed for Dominic.

'I didn't know.' She looked at her own taut fingers over the newel post and shook her head, then laughed, a small breathless sound that fluttered away after a second or two. 'It seems I'm learning more about this family today than I can cope with!' She hastily silenced what had obviously been going to be another expression of sympathy, and smiled ruefully. 'I hope you won't say anything to anyone about what you saw in the office, Jenny—please.'

'Not even to Jules?'

Naturally she would tell Jules, Bryony realised. They had no secrets from each other. 'I can't very well say not, can I?' she said. 'But no one else, Jenny, please, especially Tim.'

She tried to think why she should feel so much like crying suddenly, when she had no real reason to. Except that she could not forget how close she had come to being lost to that earthy, breathtaking magic of Dominic's, and how relieved he had professed himself to be when Jenny had broken the spell. The laugh she gave caught and died in her throat, making her shake her head impatiently.

'You heard what Dom said,' she reminded Jenny. 'You timed your entrance perfectly and saved him from

getting involved in something we'd both have regretted!'

'Oh, Bryony dear!'

Jenny didn't believe her, and Bryony couldn't bear
the look of sympathy in her eyes, so she turned swiftly
and ran up the rest of the stairs, leaving Jenny staring
after her with a dark, unhappy look in her eyes. One
kiss, and not even a proper kiss at that, should not be
allowed to cause such upheaval, and she could not
imagine why she was allowing it to. She had her hand
on the door handle when she heard a door open further
along the landing and she ducked hastily into her room.
Dominic was the last person she wanted to see at that
moment.

'I'm quite looking forward to seeing this friend of
yours.' Tim was hunched up beside her on the sand, a
length of sea-grass poked between his teeth while he
gazed out at the sea with his eyes narrowed against the
glare. 'Is she pretty?'

It was hard to believe that she had known Marion
for so long and yet she and Tim had never met, and
Bryony pondered on the definite division between her
two worlds for a moment before she answered. Pushing
her bare feet deeper into the sand, she wriggled her
toes so that the fine grains ran between them and
tickled, warm and gritty on her skin.

'She's nice and she's good-looking.' It also surprised
her to realise just how much at a loss she was when it
came to actually describing Marion's physical appearance. 'I suppose you *could* say she was pretty in a way,
but handsome is closer to the mark, I would say.'

'Flattering!' He grinned at her good-naturedly and

pushed the hat he wore further to the back of his head. 'You don't do a very good public relations job, do you?'

'Do I need to?'

Tim laughed, his eyes crinkled against the glare on the water, rolling the grass stem in his fingers. 'I thought you might have ideas about getting me interested—as a way of doing Dom's dirty work for him, and breaking me away from Sarah.'

'Tim, you know I wouldn't!'

'I'm not so sure.' Between their light brown lashes, his grey eyes regarded her steadily for a moment. 'Lately you two seem to have got——' His French mother showed in the way he used his hands, so explicit and so expressive, just as Dom did. 'You used to stand up against Dom on principle, but lately you seem to have become almost submissive, and you never seem to face up now.'

'Maybe I'm growing up.' Bryony tugged at a piece of grass and put it between her lips, rolling the hard dry stem round and round with her tongue as she stared out at the glittering surface of the ocean where a trading schooner skimmed by the shallows in a brisk wind. 'Or maybe I don't have to fight any more.'

'Hmm!' He reminded her so much of Dominic when he did that that she once more marvelled at how many small characteristics the two of them had in common. 'They come today, don't they? Ready for the festivities tomorrow. I'm surprised Dom allowed you to invite them for so long, you know how he is about people coming here as a rule.'

'I've never asked to have anyone here before!' Her swift and unmistakably defensive retort brought a grimace from Tim that she found discomfiting, and she once more sought the distraction of the passing schooner while he frowned at her curiously.

'Did you ever know him ask anyone here? Or encourage anyone else to?'

'Jules brought Jenny before they were married!' She remembered what Jenny had confided to her about that visit, and hastily dismissed the disturbing possibilities it aroused.

'Exactly!' Tim declared, bent on making his point. 'The only people the old Laminaires imported were their slaves and their wives, and I sometimes think Dom would like to see it all come back to that!'

'Oh, Tim, stop it!' She turned and looked at him, her eyes dark and unhappy because she did not understand his present mood, and his attack on Dominic least of all. 'We both owe Dom a great deal, me especially, I know, but you too. When Father died he could quite easily have sent us both packing to some convenient relations in England, but he didn't! You must be fair!'

She had touched his conscience, she knew it from the way he avoided her eyes suddenly, and concentrated on the grass that twirled between his fingers instead. Then he looked up at her, eyes crinkled and shiny in his tanned face, and as irresistible as only Tim could be.

'All right,' he conceded, without for a minute losing sight of his cause, 'but you must admit that he doesn't normally like having his little kingdom invaded, and the fact that he's letting you have friends over for several days is therefore out of character. To me it's obvious he's got something up his sleeve.'

It was difficult not to put another reason to him for

Dominic having Marion and Edward to stay, for she was used to confiding in Tim, and looking down at her hands as they dug into the sand, she laughed a little uncertainly.

'I suppose it hasn't occurred to you that he might have another reason than hoping Marion will lure you away from your Sarah?' she asked, and Tim frowned at her curiously. 'Hasn't it occurred to you that he might want to keep an eye on me and Ned Fuller?'

Tim stared at her for a moment without answering, obviously giving it serious consideration. 'Good grief!' he breathed after a moment or two. 'He didn't say so, did he?'

Dominic had said so, quite frankly, but Bryony had no intention of letting Tim know that much, and she laughed and shook her head again. 'I just don't see why you should think it's entirely for your sake that Marion and Ned are coming!'

'But suppose it was to keep an eye on you with Ned Fuller that he's encouraging this get-together; wouldn't you mind?'

Bryony drew a large circle in the sand and added points, like the rays of a sun radiating from it. 'I might,' she admitted, 'if I thought he meant it, but quite frankly I don't think Dom is that interested in what Ned Fuller does, serious or not.' She laughed, tossing back her copper-red hair and scuffing out the drawing she had done. 'But for all I know he considers Ned an ideal match for me.'

'Matchmaking, you mean?'

She knew it would be completely against Dominic's nature to indulge in anything of that nature, and she thought Tim knew it too, that was why he looked so doubtful, though not entirely sure either way. But she shrugged as if she at least considered the possibility of it.

'Maybe, I don't know. He might be glad to get me off his hands, as the saying goes!'

There was a look in Tim's eyes that gave him a shrewd, sharp look reminiscent of the father she barely remembered. 'Your Aunt Germyn was well off the mark, then, with those hints about Dom having——' Those expressive hands were disturbing in their explicitness. 'Ideas?'

If only she had not coloured so obviously and with Tim's eyes on her, or that he was not so quick to form a conclusion, she could have passed it off with more assurance. As it was there was a different air about him when he reached across and covered one of her hands with his, and his eyes were serious.

'Bry, you're not thinking of going back to England as your aunt suggested, are you? I mean—there's no reason for you to?'

'No, of course not!' She got to her feet with more haste than elegance, brushing sand from her clothes with hands that were much too unsteady, and glancing at her wristwatch as she did so. 'Good heavens, no wonder I'm so hungry! Come on, I'll race you back to the house!'

Bryony sat in the jeep beside Tim, who was perched up on the top of the seat to be able to see better and shading his eyes as she was herself, watching the progress of a cabin cruiser coming on down the shoreline towards the quay.

'Is this them?'

Bryony knelt on the seat, dazzled by the gleaming white hull as it skimmed through the water, handled with a panache that made her pretty certain it was Edward Fuller at the helm, and after a second or two, she nodded.

'It's them!'

Tim looked down at her and grinned as the cruiser was brought into the quay under Louis's dark and critical eye. 'Lovely way to show off,' he remarked mischievously. 'Your Ned looks like a bit of a swash-buckler!'

Bryony made no answer, refusing to be drawn, climbing out of the jeep as the mooring lines were flung ashore and caught by willing hands. Edward looked as smooth and charming as she remembered him, though perhaps not quite so good-looking, unless comparing him with Tim put him at a disadvantage; both her brothers were very good-looking.

Marion was dressed for the crossing, in white slacks and a bright blue tee-shirt that flattered her vivid colouring, and she looked tall and confident as she came ashore, accepting Tim's eagerly offered assistance with a smile and a glowing glance from her dark eyes. Edward, looking slightly darker than she remembered him in a white shirt and slacks, lost no time. He came ashore in one long, clean athletic stride and took Bryony's hands in his.

'Bryony!' He raised her hands one at a time to his lips and kissed her fingers. 'You look stunning in that dress!'

It was ice-green and sleeveless, with a low neck that showed off a good deal of her golden tan, and Bryony had felt good in it as soon as she put it on. Noting that

Tim was giving most of his attention to Marion, she smiled up at Edward and shook back her hair.

'It's new,' she said. 'I'm glad you like it.'

'A birthday dress?'

She shook her head, feeling wonderfully lighthearted suddenly, and Edward was holding her hand, a searching appreciative gaze scanning her face. 'My birthday isn't until tomorrow, but Dom thought it would be much better if you and Marion came over today.'

'Good of him!'

'How is Dominic?' Marion's enquiry cut across her brother's obviously sarcastic comment, and her air of familiarity with his brother's name brought a swift glance of enquiry from Tim.

'Oh, he's fine, Marion, thanks. We all are!' Bryony led the way to the jeep parked at the end of the sheds and apologised for the lack of ceremony. 'I'm afraid there's only the jeep; we don't have any call for a car on an island this size. All the driving we do is purely functional!'

Louis brought the cases over and put them on the rack at the back of the jeep, catching Bryony's eye as he did so and lifting a brow in the direction of Tim with Marion. There was no mistaking his meaning and she hastily avoided his eyes, unwilling to make her feelings known one way or the other.

It seemed a foregone conclusion that Marion should sit in the front with Tim while Bryony occupied the back seat with Edward, and equally natural that his arm should curve lightly about her shoulders as Tim started the engine and they set off along the coast road to the house.

It was a pleasant enough ride past the tall fringed

banana groves, but to Bryony it had too much familiarity to cause comment, and she thought nothing of the idea of all of it belonging to Dominic and, indirectly, to her and her brothers.

She noticed Tim glance over his shoulder at Marion and smile, being as charming as he knew how, Bryony realised, and did not know whether or not to accept it at its face value. 'You don't know our island, do you, Marion?'

'It's wonderful to think it all belongs to one family!' Marion was quite equal to the occasion, and she gave him a smile that was unmistakably encouraging. 'It's real king-of-the-castle stuff, isn't it? Imagine the Laminaires ruling this little plot for three hundred years—it's fabulous!'

Tim took the bait, smiling and charming as ever, his good-looking face turned far more often in the direction of his front seat passenger than to the road. 'I'll show you the whole thing before you go back,' he promised. 'You can drive over most of it, you know, and the rest is easily walkable.'

'Lovely!'

Tim swung the jeep round in front of the house and gallantly handed Marion out of her seat, a service that Edward performed for Bryony with even more attention and retaining his hold on her hand as they followed the other two into the house.

'I'm looking forward to the next few days,' he confessed, in a voice he kept low and deliberately intimate, she suspected. 'I've been longing to see you again, Bryony.'

Tim and Marion had gone into the *salon* where the rest of the family awaited them, leaving the door open

behind them for Bryony and Edward to follow, but
Edward held her back, his hold on her too firm to be
denied. Squeezing her fingers, he looked down into her
face with a look in his eyes that brought a faint flush of
colour to her cheeks.

'While Tim's busy with Marion, you'll be *my* guide,
won't you, Bryony?' His voice was low and quiet, and
her pulses responded to it no matter how she tried to
control them. 'You'll show me your island, won't you?'

She could see from the corner of her eye that Tim
was already introducing Marion to Jules and Jenny,
and she was uneasily conscious that they were equally
in full view to the people in the *salon*. But Edward was
bent on one thing only, and he turned her face to him
with a hand under her chin.

'Bryony?'

'Yes, of course I'll show you the island, Ned.' She
took a hasty glance at the cool room and stirred uneasily. 'You'd better come and meet the family,' she
said. 'You haven't met my other brother, Jules, and his
wife, have you?'

'No.' The brown eyes had a bright challenging look
that she thought she remembered from their last meeting. 'I've only met your third brother, Dominic.'

'My *step*brother, Ned!'

She felt a flick of resentment that he should so soon
raise that same controversy, and the set of her mouth
told him he had erred. Without hesitation he bent his
head and pressed a kiss to her lips, smiling into her eyes
as he did so. 'Ah, yes,' he said. 'I remember, you told
me so several times, didn't you?'

Bryony nodded, catching her breath when she saw
Dominic's tall lean figure coming across the *salon*, and

she remembered his reaction the last time he had seen Edward kiss her. 'It's a pleasure to see you again, Mr Fuller—welcome to Petitnue!'

He had a hand outstretched which a rather dazed Edward took automatically, and he was smiling, but when Bryony looked up and caught his eye, she saw the dark, stormy grey look of anger in them that was beginning to be all too familiar, and she discreetly avoided holding Edward's hand as they walked together into the *salon* to join the others. Having visitors for her birthday could prove more eventful than she had bargained for, and she wondered if she was going to regret issuing that impulsive invitation after all.

CHAPTER SEVEN

BRYONY had enjoyed her birthday, perhaps more than she had expected to if she was honest, and Marie had done them proud with the dinner she had prepared. A whole variety of Bryony's favourite French and Creole dishes had followed one after the other, culminating in a magnificent concoction of fresh fruits, meringue and cream, which Marie had named, with a flourish, *La Belle Laminaire*. The fact that it was presumably named in her honour and that Bryony was not a Laminaire was not questioned, except possibly by a brief glance that passed between Marion and her brother.

Tim was so obviously taken with Marion that Bryony wondered if perhaps Dominic *had* intended her to take

Tim's mind off Sarah Bryant. Once or twice she had
tried to judge how true it was, but Dominic had merely
smiled at her with those unfathomable grey eyes and
left her no wiser.

Edward was frankly interested in no one but Bryony,
and monopolised her in the same way that Tim did
Marion. With Jules and Jenny an already established
pair that seemed to leave Dominic as the odd man out,
and the idea troubled her occasionally when she
thought about it. When she mentioned it once to Tim,
however, when he came to refill his own and Marion's
glass, he laughed and suggested that Dominic should
either have invited someone of his own, or let him ask
Sarah.

'Tim, you know he couldn't! Let you invite Sarah,
I mean.'

'Not good enough, you think?'

'I mean she wouldn't have been at ease in the circumstances, and you know very well she wouldn't,
Tim! Knowing what we do, and——'

'You mean knowing that she's just about the same
number of years older than me than Dom is older than
you, one less in fact!'

Her colour rose swiftly, burning in her cheeks as she
looked at him with reproachful eyes. 'You're being
stupid, Tim, and not very nice, when you know this is
my birthday party!'

'Sorry, Bry, but I'm not getting at you as much as
Dom!' Malice lurked behind his good-natured grin,
and he stood holding two wine glasses up to the light
so that the liquid in them gleamed richly and satisfy-
ingly. 'One thing, though, I owe him thanks for having
Marion here—she's not bad.'

'I'm sure she's flattered.'

He laughed, nudging her with an elbow and almost spilling one of the drinks. 'And Ned's gaga about you. Dom's noticed that too, in case you didn't know; you'll be next for the stern guardian treatment if you're not careful!'

'Tim——'

'My lady awaits!'

He went off leaving Bryony with a hand to her neck, fingering the jewelled pendant that was Dominic's birthday gift to her. It was the first time he had ever given her jewellery and she had been thrilled with the small gold filigree leaf set with a diamond dewdrop. It was, she felt, an acknowledgement of the fact that he saw her as a woman at last and no longer as a child, and it pleased her more than she would have believed possible.

The pendant rested where the jade green silk dress she wore curved below the shadowy vee of her breast, light and cool on her soft skin and a constant reminder of its donor. And once more she looked across at Dominic, leaning back in his chair and chatting with Marion and Jules while Jenny listened, seemingly preoccupied with her own thoughts.

She could not see Edward, but while she still toyed with the jewel at her breast he leaned from behind her and spoke close to her ear. 'It's rather unusual, isn't it?'

With the delicate leaf shape between thumb and forefinger, Bryony looked down at the bright dazzle of the diamond drop, turning it so that it threw off shafts of rainbow light. 'It's beautiful,' she said softly, and wondered if Edward could have any idea of how much it had meant for her to get such a gift from Dominic, such an admission that she was grown-up at last.

'Of course it's not really a brotherly kind of present, I wouldn't have thought, but very flattering, I'm sure.' He came around to face her and she could see the way his eyes gleamed between their brown lashes while one finger traced an imaginary line from her ear to the vulnerable softness of her throat. He was smiling too, in a way that made her heart flutter. 'Diamonds *are* a girl's best friend, aren't they, Bryony?'

'I think the design is lovely.' She sounded breathless and wished she didn't, for the fact seemed to intrigue him. 'It's so very simple really, and yet it's so beautiful. Just a leaf with a dewdrop on it, or maybe a——' She broke off there, and caught her breath, remembering something suddenly that had lain forgotten in the back of her mind until now, and now gave an even deeper meaning to the gift.

Years ago when she had first come to Petitnue, before her father died even, she had come out into the garden after a rain storm and discovered what to her had seemed a miracle of beauty. On one of the garden shrubs a brown skeleton leaf eaten by insects had somehow survived the beating rain and winds and still clung to its stem, with a single raindrop shimmering on its hair-fine veins.

She had stood and gazed at it for a long time, she remembered, and when she heard someone coming, turned quickly, anxious for whoever it was to share her wonder. Seeing Dominic she had expected impatience, perhaps even scorn, but instead he had seemed as enchanted as she was herself, crouching down beside her with an arm about her shoulders while they watched the single drop of moisture shimmer and gleam in the sunlight with rainbow colours, just as the diamond did. It was, she thought, the first time she had been consciously aware of Dominic's gentleness, and she had never told another soul about their shared miracle.

It was instinctive to seek him where he sat relaxed and at ease, using his hands to emphasise some point he was making, and her heart beat with a stronger more urgent beat as she watched him. Then, as if he sensed her watching, he turned his head and looked at the filigree leaf with its diamond raindrop nestled against her skin, before raising his eyes.

He recognised her sudden realisation and he smiled; a smile that showed in his eyes rather than on his mouth and, pressing the precious reminder to her breast, she held his gaze, her own eyes huge and brilliant as blue gems while her lips formed his name. 'Dom!' so softly that not even Edward heard.

'Hey!' Edward waved a hand in front of her face, laughing and looking deep into her eyes, so that she could no longer see Dominic. 'What happened? You suddenly went off into a trance and looked all starry-eyed!' An arm encircled her shoulders and he hugged her with the familiarity she was beginning to expect from him now. 'Maybe you need a change of scene, eh? Let's go and explore the gardens and take in the moon-light, shall we?'

The moment was gone; that magic moment when she seemed to see into Dominic's heart, and she resented Edward's having shattered it. But Dominic was once more involved in conversation, as if he had never been distracted from it, and Edward was waiting to walk with her in the moonlight. The gold leaf with its soli-tary tear had probably been intended as no more than a pleasant reminder of a childish pleasure, and she had been silly to suppose it was meant as anything else.

'It's going to rain, Ned.' She managed to sound quite matter-of-fact and Edward's brown eyes gleamed with speculation, his smile confident.

'Not yet, it isn't,' he assured her, as if he knew with certainty. 'Come on, Bryony, we can always scoot back to the house if it starts.'

The persuasive arm about her shoulders urged her towards the door, and she really had no reason not to go with him. It wasn't raining yet, and she had said more than once how much she liked the gardens at night, when the crickets chirruped, and friendly little lizards scuttled away into the undergrowth to watch you with hooded eyes.

Smiling up at Edward, she nodded. 'All right, I'll come, but we mustn't go far.'

'No, ma'am!'

Laughing, he bent and kissed her mouth, satisfied to have got his way, but Bryony was aware as she went with him of Dominic watching them go and almost inevitably thinking how easily they could be caught if a storm started.

The paths wound about the bushes in a tortuous maze, making the distance twice as far, and giving the impression of complete isolation as giant hibiscus, pouis and frangipani sprang up between them and the house. It was possible to go a long way without realising just how far, and they had gone nearly half a kilometre, close to where the groves began, before they paused.

It was the kind of evening when everything seemed to be standing still. Even the winds had dropped and only the slightest movement stirred the jacaranda leaves above Bryony's head. The air was sultry and heavy with the promise of rain, but it was the rainy season and by now she was accustomed to the fact that the months that brought most rain coincided with the period when the breathtaking flora of the Caribbean was at its lush and exotic best. The one feature was dependent upon the other, and it was a small price to pay.

The air was heavy and oppressive away from the artificially cooled air indoors, and there was that curious, almost exciting sense of anticipation in the atmosphere that always preceded a storm. She felt sticky and hot and, leaning back against the trunk of the jacaranda, she looked up at the small patch of night sky visible to her through the feathery leaves and clusters of blue bell-like flowers.

The moon was hidden and scrolls of cloud frowned down at them, seeming barely to skim the tree-tops, dark and threatening with a ghostly shimmer of silver edging each black scroll, etched there by the escaping moonlight.

A chittering cricket seemed to sense the approaching storm and kept up his squeaky anxious warning until silenced suddenly, as if his own concern in anything at all had been abruptly cut off. It was hot, oppressively so, and Bryony felt her body droop limply as she leaned back her head, trying to dismiss the intrusive memory of an eleven-year-old girl with a miracle to share.

A child sharing a magic moment with the man who, less than a year later, was to become her guardian and who, after all these years, had given her a beautiful and extravagant reminder of that moment, for her birthday gift. She wished she understood him as easily as she understood Edward Fuller, whose motives were never in any doubt.

Edward was close beside her, resting against the same tree and with the last short length of a cigarette burning between his fingers. It was his action of treading the smouldering end out underfoot that drew her attention to him, and she smiled vaguely.

The evening darkness gave him a look of mystery that betrayed nothing of what was going on in his mind, but she needed little intelligence to guess. Nevertheless she drew an involuntary breath when he slid an arm around behind her and drew her away from the support of the tree so that he could look down into her face, and she thought he smiled.

'It's hot!'

It reminded her that he had spent the past few years in England at university, and that he was probably still acclimatising, and she nodded. 'You feel it more, I expect, having been away for a few years.'

'Maybe.'

She could sense something of the same taut anticipation and excitement in the encircling arm, and in the body that barely touched hers as he held her, as there was in her own. The anticipation of a storm aroused almost the same disturbing violence in human reaction as it did in the elements, she thought.

Glancing up at the cloudy sky, she eased out of his embrace, trying to make the move as little like a rejection as possible, but standing with her back to him and looking along the path to the tall, ragged fronds of banana at the beginning of the groves.

'It will be a relief when the storm breaks, and at least this time no one's out in it. You're not worried about your boat, are you, Ned?' She knew the question was unnecessary, but she asked it just the same, switching her gaze quickly in the direction of the house when the first warning roll of thunder grumbled angrily out at sea. 'Louis will see to the moorings if it blows up too hard, though I don't think it will.'

Edward left the tree and slid an arm around her once more, a smile on his mouth as he took care she should not evade him this time. His hold was tighter and his fingers curved firmly into her waist as he pulled her close against him.

'I'm not worried about anything, except that you don't seem to be enjoying my company very much.' He had gained such a hold on her that she could not even move, and his voice was close to her ear, his breath warm on her neck. 'You aren't trying to escape me, are you, Bryony?'

It wasn't only the effect of the stormy atmosphere, Bryony realised; they had probably all had rather more wine than they would normally drink. The timbre of Edward's voice certainly suggested that his usual smooth self-confidence had been further boosted by champagne and the various table wines that Marie had served with dinner.

Without quite understanding her reason, Bryony wanted to be free of that unyielding arm, but she was unwilling at the moment to make an issue of it, so she did no more than use her hands to slightly ease the firm hold on her waist.

'I'm not trying to escape, Ned, nothing so dramatic, but it's very hot, and you're not making it any more comfortable by squeezing me so tightly.'

'Don't you like being squeezed?'

He pulled his arm so tightly around her that she caught her breath and struggled against him. 'Ned, you hurt, don't do that!'

'Oh, Bryony!'

His laughter sounded close to her ear, and he bent his head to kiss her neck, a light soft caress that sent little shivers down the length of her spine. Then he turned her within the curve of his arm and held her facing him, both arms clasping her tightly to make sure she did not elude him. His eyes had a glowing darkness that was almost black in the stormy light, and she glimpsed just the slightest gleam of white between his lips, as if his smile was tight-lipped rather than the broad confident beam it usually was.

'I never saw such a girl for making excuses not to be kissed! It's your birthday—come on and enjoy it!'

Her hands were flat against his chest and she could feel the increased beat of his heart and smell the masculine scent he used, made more powerful by the heat of his body, as she held against the determined strength of his arms about her. He had never left his intention in any doubt, and she had no one to blame but herself, but all the same the situation was unwelcome and she wished she could see some way out of it.

Edward Fuller was young and good-looking and reasonably wealthy; he was the brother of her closest friend and she liked him quite a lot, and yet she did not want to be in his arms. She did not want him to become as amorous as the look in his eyes showed her he wanted to be.

The storm was closer now and she saw it as a possible means of ending the situation without having to resort to personal rejection. The sky was ripped open with great gashes of lightning and the rumbling growl of thunder moved nearer every second, and she knew they must be going; should have gone before this if they were to get back to the house before the rain came.

'Ned, it's time we went back—the storm's getting close and it's quite a long way to go.'

'It's not here yet!' He sounded almost savage in his determination, and she tried once more to ease away from him. 'Oh, come on, Bryony, let yourself relax and have fun!'

His arms tightened and his face came closer, looming over her and alarmingly unfamiliar, so that she instinctively turned away to avoid the mouth that would have descended on hers. There was a tense urgency in the arms that held her that seemed to echo the approaching fury of the storm, and she tried once more to free herself.

'Ned, please, we——'

When she turned her face to speak to him, he took immediate advantage of it and sought her mouth unerringly, taking her by surprise so that for a second or so she became passive, almost responsive, to his kiss. When he let her go she felt too breathless to do anything other than shake her head, while she stood with her hands tightly curled against the softness of his shirt.

'You don't dislike me, do you?'

The question was half-teasing, but yet she thought it had an underlying seriousness. It would be difficult for Edward to believe anyone could actually dislike him, she guessed, but he was puzzled by her reluctance to let him have his way, and she supposed it was her own fault that he laboured under the obvious delusion. She had agreed to come out there with him and he had left his intention in little doubt.

Instead of breaking contact with him completely, she simply leaned back against his arms and looked at the slightly sulky mouth as she sought to explain. 'You know I don't dislike you, Ned, I wouldn't have asked you to come here with Marion if I did.'

'But you don't like me kissing you!'

'I didn't——' She broke off abruptly when the sky above them seemed to erupt—a huge slash of lightning followed immediately by a thunderous roar that seemed to shake the very ground beneath their feet. 'Ned, we must go!'

'Bryony——'

'We must, Ned, we'll get soaked as it is!'

He hated to yield, even now, she thought, but he had no option. The rain came suddenly, as it always did; a heavy, soaking deluge that tapped and hissed on the leaves around them, channelled as if down a chute from the jacaranda leaves to add to the downpour. It pounded the path and swished about their feet in fury. Her dress was thin and Bryony fervently wished they had not come so far from the house, when all the signs had been that a storm was due.

Edward took her hand, pulling her along with him as he ran, along the path towards the warm glow of light that was the house, winding round and between shrubs and trees that brushed their faces and shoulders with wet leaves and added to the deluge.

'Ned!'

She caught her foot and went sprawling on the path, face down with the wind knocked out of her and the coolness of rain soaking through her thin dress. She lay there until hands reached down to haul her to her feet, hasty impatient hands that took no account of the fact that she was not only winded but grazed, and she once more stumbled along in his wake, shaking the wet hair from her face.

She had lost a shoe and for a second or two she stumbled over the remaining high heel that threw her completely off balance. 'Ned!' She hopped on one leg trying to take off the other shoe. 'Ned, wait, please!'

He turned his face to her, dark and streaming wet, lit by vivid flashes of lightning that slashed jaggedly back and forth across the sky, ripping great gashes in the overcast of clouds, and his eyes were black and questioning.

'What's wrong, Bryony?'

Impatience edged his voice and she resented it. 'I've lost a shoe and I can't keep my balance.'

'Then take off the other one!'

He let go her hand and she did as he said, her discomfort making his manner even less acceptable, so that she stopped to wonder why she had thought Ned Fuller smoothly charming when he could prove so cavalier at a time like this. He took her hand again as soon as she had dispensed with the other shoe and she was once more taken along without really having much option.

There wasn't much further to go, just past the next clump of hibiscus, shining like fragrant wet stars in the light from the house windows, but the familiar path had never seemed so long before and she was panting with the exertion of running faster than she was normally capable of.

'Ned, I can't keep up!'

Her voice had been pitched to be heard above the ear-splitting shriek of thunder, and in the following lull it sounded shrill and urgent as she sought to free herself from Edward's hold. A movement just ahead of them caught her eye and a moment later Dominic appeared out of the streaming darkness, illuminated from behind by the house lights. The thunder roared in the wake of another ragged lightning flash so that his arrival seemed almost theatrical in its drama, and she stared at him.

His raincoat was barely wet, she noticed, so he could only just have left the house, and she wondered why he was out at all; Louis could check the moorings and there was nothing anyone could do about possible damage to the crops until it was all over. Without a word he came on down the path to meet them, snatching her hand from Edward's and lifting her into his arms in almost the same movement.

'I lost my shoes and——'

'Save it!'

The instruction was curt and abrupt and Bryony bit her lip on the rest of her explanation; obviously he was not interested, but he *was* angry. With one arm about his neck she was thrillingly aware of the strength of him, and of the fierce, hot passion that made every muscle taut and hard as steel.

Edward didn't argue; perhaps he was too anxious to gain shelter himself, or perhaps he had seen that look of Dominic's and decided against explanations at this point. He hurried on into the house with Dominic only a step or two behind him carrying Bryony in his arms, wet and bedraggled and showing blood on both knees.

He set her down carefully on the floor and her bare

feet curled involuntarily at the cool smooth touch of the tiles. She kept one hand on him, flat-palmed and pressed to the dampness of his shoulder, as if she did not want to lose the touch of him.

'Are you badly hurt?' The grey eyes were storm-dark and she hastily avoided them because of the response they brought from her senses. She shook her head without saying anything, merely looking down at the grazed flesh of her knees that still bled a little and looked probably much more serious than it was. 'Marie will put something on for you as soon as you've dried off.'

'I can see to it, Dom, I——'

'Just for once do as you're told, Bryony!'

A bristle of resentment brought her chin up and she looked at him for a second with bright blue eyes that showed how she felt. She sensed Edward move where he stood at the foot of the stairs, and spoke hastily to forestall any protest he might think of making, not knowing whether he intended one or not.

'I'll get Marie to find me some balm after I've washed them clean—I can manage *that* myself.'

He simply nodded, then gave his attention to Edward, a swift raking glance that noted the condition of the once smart and expensive suit he had worn for the celebration dinner. 'I'll see that Marie finds you extra towels and get her to do something about your suit.' He raised his voice. 'Marie!'

Marie appeared almost at once, her face wrinkled with concern when she saw Bryony, and murmuring softly in her own tongue she took her arm, barely sparing a glance for Edward. 'Come, *petite*, Marie make you better, *hein*?'

Marie had never learned to treat her any differently, and to Bryony her maternal fussing was sometimes quite welcome, like now, when she felt sore and bedraggled and quite certain that Dominic was only waiting a more opportune moment before wanting to know how she had hurt herself.

'See that Mr Fuller has extra towels, and try and do something about his suit, will you, Marie?'

Edward looked ruefully at his soaking wet clothes and pulled a face. 'I'm afraid it's beyond redemption,' he mourned, but Marie was shaking her head as she hustled both her charges towards the stairs.

'I'll fix him,' she promised cheerfully. 'Good as new!'

Obviously from Edward's face he did not share her confidence, but he made no argument, merely glancing at Bryony before he took the lead. Unable to resist it, Bryony glanced back over her shoulder to where Dominic was stripping off his raincoat. Flinging it down on to a chair, after a token shake to remove some of the wet, he looked up suddenly and caught her eye, but his expression was unsmiling and it was impossible to read anything in the eyes so carefully hidden by thick dark lashes. It was hard to believe he was jealous, and yet the thought persisted as she followed Edward and Marie upstairs.

Stripped and towelled dry, she felt much better, and she answered Marie's knock quite cheerfully, smiling to counteract her anxious expression. 'I'm all right, Marie, really— I was just wet, that's all.'

'An' you got hurt.' Marie pointed to her grazed knees that still looked tender and bled a little, and she was shaking her head and clucking reproachfully as she bent to take a closer look. 'I don' know what we gon' do with you, *petite*!'

'I'm not a child, Marie!'

Marie said nothing, but gave her attention to dressing the wounds while Bryony sat on the bathroom stool and watched her. It still surprised her to realise how uncaring Edward had been when she fell, and she pondered on whether or not she had been rather spoiled by the unusually gentle way her two brothers treated her. Even Dominic had been concerned for all his impatience with her; concerned enough to carry her back to the house.

'Dom's going to be *very* sarcastic about this,' she remarked, and Marie nodded solemnly.

'You should have known better, *petite*, to go out so far when dey a storm brewin' an' everyone knows it.' The dark eyes glanced up at her curiously, no attempt made to disguise the speculation going on behind them. 'I 'spose dat young man made you lose your sense, eh?' Her wrinkled golden face creased briefly in a knowing smile and her eyes gleamed. 'He pretty good-lookin', ain't he?'

Bryony took it in good part, though she knew Marie would never have taken similar liberties with Dominic, but she wished she need not have coloured up as if she had some cause to blush. Nothing had passed between her and Edward that warranted blushing over, whether Marie believed it or not; although it might have been different if Edward had had his way.

'He's very nice.' She began brushing her still damp hair, not looking at Marie. 'But you're on the wrong track, Marie, thinking along those lines.'

'*Peut-être*,' Marie shrugged, taking the brush from

her and using it vigorously on her copper-red hair, watching her face in the mirror as she did so. 'Monsieur Laminaire think along those lines—he think you crazy to go so far when it gon' to storm!'

'Well, it's got nothing to do with him whether there is or not!' Tossing back her hair, Bryony walked away from the ministering brush and went back into her bedroom for a last look in the mirror before she went back downstairs. 'I'm not a little girl any longer, you know, Marie, I grew up!'

Marie followed her, brush in hand, looking at the slim soft shape in a pale silk dress with the gold leaf glowing against warm scented skin, the diamond raindrop catching the light and flashing its rainbow heart. Copper-red hair framed a small face from which huge blue eyes watched her almost warily via the brightly lit mirror, and Marie wore a curious half-smile on her mouth.

'You think he don' know that?' she asked, and Bryony turned swiftly away.

The pendant swung against her breast and she held it in the palm of her hand for a second, feeling the glowing raindrop stone pressing into her skin. 'I think he's beginning to,' she said half to herself.

Downstairs once more she found Edward, changed from his elegant fawn suit into a white shirt and slacks, but there was no sign of Dominic and she automatically sent an enquiring glance at Jules. He sat with Marion on the divan, a situation that Tim, on the other side of her, obviously took a poor view of, judging by his expression.

Seeing her, Jules smiled encouragingly. 'Hello, sweetheart, feeling O.K. after your ducking?'

'You must have been crackers going out so far when there was a storm in the offing,' Tim declared frankly. 'You deserved to get soaked!'

Ignoring him, Bryony took a chair next to Jenny, then looked across at Edward who gave the appearance of feeling slightly sheepish, as if he was doubtful about the reception she was going to give him. Catching his eye, she smiled, wondering as she did so if perhaps he regretted having shown her a more ruthless side to his character.

'You're none the worse, are you, Ned?'

'Good as new!' His smile lacked only a little of its usual confidence, and he drew on the cigarette he held before he said any more. 'How are your legs? Sorry, but I didn't even realise you'd hurt yourself until—your brother picked you up. You must have thought me a callous brute for hauling you along the way I did, but you should have said something.'

'Oh, it isn't much.' It was too close to the truth for her to feel comfortable about denying it outright, so she compromised. 'I just thought you were anxious to get in out of the rain.'

'What *did* happen, Bryony?'

From Marion's question it was safe to assume that the same query asked of Edward had drawn blank, which was not surprising since he professed to have known nothing about her hurting herself until Dominic picked her up in his arms and carried her. But she wondered if it could, in part at least, account for Dominic's anger, if he had seen Edward hauling her along as he had with her knees bleeding, and shoeless through the pouring rain.

'Oh, it was my own fault really.' She used her hands

airily, as if to deprive the words of too much importance. 'I know the ground and Ned doesn't. I should have had more sense than to walk so far when I knew there was rain about.'

'But how did you hurt your knees?'

Edward was frowning and she thought that in other circumstances he would have told his sister to stop asking questions that could embarrass him; instead he sat with his hands together, his cigarette burning away in the ashtray beside him while Bryony explained further.

'When the storm caught us we had to run, as you can imagine, and those high heels I was wearing were hardly made for running. Ned was holding my hand and pulling me along behind him, not realising I couldn't keep up, and eventually I lost one shoe, which made matters worse.' She laughed and shook her head. 'Anyway, I fell flat on my face in a most undignified manner, and grazed both my knees!'

Marion was nodding her head and there was an unmistakable gleam in her dark eyes, as if she could picture it all too easily. 'I rather think Dominic thought the worst when he saw the state you were in,' she told Bryony, ignoring her brother's quick frown when she said it. 'You were so long coming after the rain started and'—she shrugged and laughed—'well, he didn't know where you were!'

A swift flush of colour warmed Bryony's cheeks once more and she lamented her tendency to blush so easily of late. Without looking at Edward, she shook her head. 'Even running as we were, it takes a very long time to get back from the plantation, and we'd left it too late before we started.' Quite instinctively she registered the appearance of Dominic's tall figure looming in the doorway, and to angle her chin the way she did was automatic; just as it was to speak as if she was still unaware of him being there. 'Anyway, I don't see that it need have concerned Dom or anyone else where we were, need it?'

Jenny caught her breath, Bryony heard it quite distinctly, and almost before the words were out of her mouth she was regretting them. Dominic said nothing, but when he came striding across in her direction she felt her heart thudding wildly, and she did not look up until he walked on past her and bent to take a cheroot from a box on the table beside Jenny. As he lit it, his hands were sure and steady, and the flame from the lighter sent small, swift shadows flicking across the strong rugged face.

It was Jules, almost inevitably, who broke the awkward silence. 'We thought you might have gone along the coast road a way, so when the rain started Dom thought it might be a good idea to take the jeep and look for you. It seemed better than letting you and Ned get soaked to the skin.'

It was difficult to know what to say, but Bryony gave a hasty glance at Dominic's dark and unrelenting face and decided to make her apology to Jules. 'I'm sorry, I didn't know.'

Jules smiled tolerantly, aware as he always was of how easy it was for her to flare up and then regret it only seconds later. He made a wry face and shook his head at her. 'I know you didn't, love, that's why I'm telling you.'

'Don't bother to explain, Jules, you'll be wasting your time with Little Miss Independence!'

The grey eyes behind a cloud of smoke were steely, and Bryony felt herself shiver. His voice, too, might have sounded no more than mildly reproachful or maybe faintly amused, but to Bryony it had the edge of hardness that she always hated to hear, and she was more than ready to back down if only he gave her the opportunity. It was a fact lately that she hated having Dominic at odds with her more than she ever had before, though she could not quite understand why it mattered so much more than it had once.

'Dom, I didn't know you were coming in the jeep to look for us. I didn't expect you to do that.'

It was a moment or two before Dominic looked at her, but when he did, she thought the grey eyes were less steely and the mouth a little more relaxed as he pursed his lips to expel smoke in a long jet. And probably no one else noticed the inward sigh of resignation, unless they were watching him with the same intentness as she was herself.

A faint lingering ghost of a smile hovered about his mouth and he looked at her steadily, regretfully almost, as if it hurt him to have her misjudge him. 'No, you wouldn't expect me to, would you, *ma petite*?' She clenched her hands tightly when he shook his head. 'That's something that saddens me.'

'Dom——'

'*Non, non, non!*' He shook his head, getting to his feet and standing for a moment to look down at her. 'Let's have more champagne, shall we? After all, it's still your birthday!'

CHAPTER EIGHT

As tomorrow was to be Marion and Edward's last day on the island, the four of them had decided to go swimming. Using aqua-lung equipment, the idea was for them to go in off Edward's cabin cruiser which would be anchored just off the shallows, and it was Bryony who suggested it might be best if they left someone on board while they were all in the water. She thought Louis would be only too pleased to join them, if Dominic could spare him, and she foresaw little difficulty in persuading him.

What she did not forsee was that it would be Marion who took the initiative and told him about their plans, before she had a chance to say anything herself. Marion had always claimed that she found him attractive, but she had never before attempted to openly flirt with him, in fact during her stay they had been rather formal in their exchanges, a situation that Dominic seemed quite happy with. Her present manner towards him showed a distinct change, even though she still addressed him by his full name.

'We're going aqua-lung diving tomorrow, Monsieur Laminaire; won't you join us?'

If the invitation surprised Dominic he gave no sign of it other than a briefly raised brow, but he responded to the unmistakable gleam in Marion's dark eyes, with a half-smile. 'Me?'

'I'm sure you'd enjoy it, and we'd love to have you.' Her gaze scanned his tall muscular frame with frank admiration. 'And I'm sure you're a marvellous swimmer.'

He was, but Dominic neither committed himself to an opinion of his own prowess nor dismissed out of hand, as Bryony expected him to, the idea of joining them. Instead he seemed prepared to let Marion persuade him, whether he meant to eventually accept or not, and seeing him so apparently responsive took Bryony unawares and brought a prickling feeling of resentment.

'I'm flattered.' he allowed.

His grey eyes gleamed with laughter, as if he recognised some ulterior motive behind the invitation. He leaned forward to tap ash from his cheroot and his voice was threaded with laughter and faintly mocking as he sought Marion's suddenly evasive eyes.

'I'm also tempted,' he admitted, and smiled directly at her when she looked up to offer further encouragement. 'And I know you refer to me as Dominic, Marion, so why not use my name now, *hein*?'

Tim cleared his throat and he was frowning; so far during her stay he had regarded himself as Marion's natural companion, and he obviously viewed Dominic's unaccustomed dalliance with suspicion. Bryony disliked the situation too, though she did her best to stifle the unfamiliar confusion of annoyance and anxiety it aroused.

Dominic was at his most French; very much the man of the world, and she could imagine the effect he was having. Mature, confident and stunningly masculine, he was more than a match for any woman, and Marion, for all her air of sophistication, was only a little older than Bryony; she could guess how she felt.

Marion's dark eyes switched to her briefly, and she saw the uncertainty there, as if she had for once been caught out of her depth. Obviously she had hoped for a response from him, but it had been rather different from what she expected. Her recovery was rapid, however, and she was smiling again, using her eyes to encourage him.

'Dominic,' she repeated obediently, and he laughed. A bright gleam in her eyes, she looked at him from the shadow of her lashes. 'Why *don't* you come with us, Dominic?'

He sat forward in his chair, elbows resting on his knees and regarding her with eyes narrowed against the smoke he expelled from pursed lips. 'I'm tempted, as I said, but unfortunately I can't spare the time.'

'Ah!' She pouted her disappointment. 'Can't you be spared for just a few hours?'

'I'm afraid not. Bryony will tell you how busy I am always.'

Marion's laughter had a soft reproachful sound and she did not look across at Bryony, but kept her eyes for Dominic only. 'But Bryony isn't asking you, I am.'

For a moment he fixed his disturbing grey eyes on her, and Bryony felt her senses respond urgently, even though she hastily avoided looking at him. 'Bryony *wouldn't* ask me,' he said quietly. 'Would you, *ma petite*?' He didn't wait for a reply, but returned his attention to Marion. 'I'd be superfluous, obviously.' His gaze took in the four of them seated about the room. 'Four is a more comfortable number and I should be the odd man out.'

A challenge lurked somewhere in that deep quiet voice, and Marion obviously recognised it, but she merely gave a swift and rather uneasy glance at Bryony and shrugged. 'Maybe,' she agreed.

'You're both good swimmers, I presume?' He obviously considered Edward as the leader of the party, for he addressed the question to him. 'Bryony and Tim are both excellent swimmers, having spent half their lives in the water, but they haven't done much aqualung diving.'

Edward's good-looking face showed self-satisfaction and he smiled, as if he was about to spring a surprise. 'I'm pretty good, I was university champion for two years running.'

'Ah!'

It was impossible to tell whether or not Dominic was impressed, he wasn't easy to impress on the whole and she thought he would be willing enough to agree that Louis should accompany them. He had always trusted Louis and she was almost certain he did not like trusting Edward to see that every precaution was taken to ensure their safety.

'There was one thing, Dom.' She spoke up before the idea became swamped in other matters. 'We need someone to stay on deck while we're swimming, and I wondered if you'd mind if Louis came with us.'

There was no doubt in Bryony's mind that it was relief she saw for a moment in his eyes before he nodded and smiled agreement. 'But of course, *petite*, I'm sure he'd love to come with you, and I'll feel easier if he's aboard—just in case anything goes wrong.' He caught her eye and briefly lowered one lid. 'But I'm glad it was you who suggested it, *ma chère*, and not me, or you'd have accused me of——' He heaved his broad shoulders in an explicit Gallic shrug and his eyes were bright with laughter. 'Heaven knows what you'd have called me!'

'No, Dom, I——'

'Wouldn't you?' he insisted, and she pursed her bottom lip, unable to deny it, while his laughter rippled through her senses like the touch of a cool finger tracing along her spine.

'I suppose so,' she admitted.

The fact that Tim seemed to have become so attached to Marion during the past few days was something that Bryony accepted gladly, although she hoped he wasn't going to spoil everything by growing jealous of her friend's unexpected attempt to flirt with Dominic, as he had showed signs of doing today.

It was to discover if she could, how Dominic felt about Tim's apparent change of heart that she had stayed on in the *salon* after everyone else had gone to bed. It was always so difficult to know just what Dominic's reactions were to any situation, until he chose to make them known, and she was curious enough to want to find out.

Tim had suggested at the beginning that Dominic's idea in asking Edward and Marion to stay for several days was in the hope that Marion would take his mind off Sarah Bryant, and she could hardly deny that the same thought had occurred to her. If that had indeed been his motive, then it showed every sign of being well planned, and it seemed reasonable enough in the circumstances to ask him.

He was curious about her lingering after the rest of them had gone to bed, but she guessed he was waiting for her to make the first move. He occupied an armchair in one corner of the room, and the *salon* had never seemed so overpoweringly big and quiet as it did now, with only the two of them left in it.

Most of the lights were out and a low lamp by Dominic's chair cast shadows across his face, leaving gaunt hollows and clefts about the strong cheeks and chin, while the grey eyes watched her from the dark depths of thick lashes as she got up from her own chair and moved restlessly about the room.

'Aren't you tired?'

She turned and looked across at him, her indecision showing in her face, and he smiled encouragingly. 'I wanted to—to talk to you, that's all.'

An arm extended, the long fingers curved invitingly, persuading her towards him where he sat in that small warm patch of light. 'Then come and talk, *ma petite*, huh?'

Bryony had never felt so self-conscious as she did during the few seconds it took her to walk across the room to him, and she felt the scrutiny of those steady grey eyes like a physical touch until he took her into the curve of his arm and drew her down on to the arm of his chair. There was a curiously unfamiliar sense of excitement being so close to him, and she was alarmingly aware of the strength of the arm that held her as well as the spicy masculine scent he used, mingled with the heat of his body.

'You—you like Marion, don't you, Dom? Now that you know her better, I mean.'

'What you mean is do I like her better than Sarah Bryant as a prospect for Tim, isn't that it?' His voice was warm with laughter and he had so accurately interpreted her reasons for asking that she hastily avoided his eyes, feeling slightly on the defensive.

'I noticed you liked her better on your own behalf!'
she retorted impulsively, and coloured furiously when
he laughed. 'I don't care about that,' she went on
hastily and a little breathlessly, 'but she and Tim are
more of an age than he and Sarah are, and Tim likes
her quite a lot.'

'Also it suits you better, doesn't it, *petite*?'

There was something in his voice that made her
frown and she got up from the arm of his chair and
walked off a way, turning to try and judge his mood.
He drew deeply on the cheroot and made a great deal
of smoke in the yellow aura of light that surrounded
him, so that it was impossible to see what was in his
eyes.

'What could be cosier,' he asked, 'than Tim safely
paired off with your friend, and you with her brother,
eh? Isn't that how you see it all working out, *ma chère*?'

Nothing had been further from her mind than herself and Edward, and she hastened to tell him so. 'No,
no, no, I hadn't thought about Ned and me, I meant
Tim and Marion! I thought you'd prefer Marion.'

'If I had the choice I wouldn't want Tim to marry
either of them,' Dominic admitted frankly. 'But I don't
have any more right to interfere in Tim's life than I do
in yours, and if it has to be one or the other I must confess I'd rather it was your friend.' A dark brow arched
quizzically. 'There, *petite*, does that satisfy you?'

She could have left it there, she realised, and perhaps
she should have done, but instead she still lingered,
her eyes searching that dark and shadowed face for
something, she wasn't sure what. It was hard for her to
forget how he had openly flirted with Marion earlier,

and she wished it didn't bother her quite so much.

'You don't think Marion would be good for Tim?'

He speculated on it for a second or two, or so it seemed to her, then he shrugged and smiled. 'Who knows? She's a very attractive girl——'

'You noticed *that*!'

'Yes, *ma chère*, I did.' He was still smiling, but there was a look in his eyes that was making her feel strangely uneasy. 'But I don't somehow see Tim being happy with her. Your friend is a very attractive girl and very, very sure of herself, but I think she might prove too much for someone as easily swayed as Tim. She's a very strong character and she needs someone with an even stronger character to handle her or he, whoever he is, will sink without trace!'

'Someone like you!'

'I didn't say that.'

'I know, but you——'

'I know that she took Tim's letter to Sarah Bryant, and not you, *petite*.' He interrupted her gently and he was smiling at her through the haze of smoke from the cheroot, shaking his head at her as he did so. 'No one could mistake your copper-red head for Marion's dark brown, and Miss Bryant described a dark girl to me.' He caught and held her gaze, his own disturbingly steady. 'I wasn't too surprised to learn that you couldn't after all bring yourself to defy me to the extent of actually delivering that letter for Tim. It took someone like Marion to take the initiative in *that*.'

Nothing she did could surprise him, she realised, and wondered why it gave her such a wonderful sense of comfort suddenly, because he knew her so well. Snuggling up in the armchair next to his, she hugged her knees and smiled at him with a hint of challenge.

'But you *did* invite Marion and Ned here so that Marion could—go to work on Tim, didn't you?'

'As well as I can follow your disgusting English, I have to admit it.' His grey eyes were laughing, gleaming warmly in a way that set her heart racing as she looked at him. 'Marion is also—working, on me, had you noticed? But yes, of course you have, you've remarked on it more than once this evening.'

He was obviously still amused by Marion's flirtatious approach earlier, and Bryony was puzzled by his attitude. 'I couldn't help noticing the way she was flirting with you when she asked if you'd like to join us tomorrow.' She lowered her lashes and concentrated on tracing an imaginary pattern on the skirt of her dress with a finger-tip. 'I noticed how you were lapping it up too.'

'*Mon dieu*, I might as well have sent you to the shack school in the village for all the good it's done for your English!' he declared in mock horror. 'As for your friend flirting with me, I have to admit I couldn't resist playing up to her—especially after last night.'

'Last night?'

'Last night when I was on my way to my bedroom I was—waylaid by Marion.' Bryony blinked at him in startled bewilderment and he laughed, sending up more smoke to haze and soften the rugged outlines of his face. 'She was on the landing of the old wing,' he explained, 'and I think she'd been waiting for me. I couldn't swear to it, but she obviously thought she might as well take advantage of the situation, accidental *or* contrived.' His grey eyes were bright with laughter and her amazement only seemed to increase his amusement. 'I've always said your friend was far more sophisticated than her years, and she rolled her eyes at me in a way there was no mistaking. Being a man, I have to admit I was tempted, however briefly.'

'Oh, Dom!' Her hands to her face, she stared at him over her fingers. 'I'd no idea she'd done anything like that. I—I only hope you weren't too embarrassed.'

Dominic leaned forward, crushing out the cheroot with his dark strong fingers, and he was obviously far from embarrassed by the incident; probably less so than she was herself. 'It was no more embarrassing for me than it is for you when Ned does the same thing.'

She wished he had not brought that matter up, and she looked at him with a hint of reproach. 'That isn't quite the same thing, I mean——'

'That I'm so much older and therefore should not expect to be—flirted with, eh? Is that it, *petite*?'

'No, of course I didn't mean that; you know I didn't, Dom!'

He dismissed her protest with a sweep of one big hand and smiled. 'I'm not embarrassed when a pretty girl flirts with me, *ma chère* and especially when I know she isn't doing it for the usual reasons.'

Bryony frowned at him curiously. It was difficult enough at any time to follow what was going on in his mind, and harder still when he sat in the shadows as he did now, with the soft light from a solitary lamp making such deceptive play over the rugged hollows of his face.

'I don't quite understand,' she confessed, and watched him raise his lean length from the armchair to tower over her.

His eyes had a depthless darkness as he looked down

at her and a ghost of smile hovered about his mouth. 'The obvious play is not for Marion's own sake,' he said in his quiet, gentle voice, 'it is for yours, Bryony. She hopes that by getting me to flirt with her, you'll be jealous enough to resent it.'

The catch of her breath was clearly audible in the big quiet room and she stared up at him with wide unbelieving eyes, her mind in chaos. 'Oh, Dom, you surely don't believe that!'

Her voice was small and strangely husky and she felt herself trembling as she responded automatically to the two large hands thrust suddenly in front of her, palms upward. She put her own into them, thrilling to the warm clasp of strong fingers as he drew her to her feet and she stood facing him.

'Come on, kitten, it's time you were in bed, or you'll never have the energy for all that swimming tomorrow.'

He still held her hands while she stood musing on whether or not Marion had meant to arouse the response that Dominic claimed. Even Edward had admitted his sister's desire to see her married to Dominic, and she had said so quite openly to Bryony herself, more than once. But the thought of her employing such an obvious strategy with someone as discerning as Dominic was embarrassing to her, however unmoved it left him.

She felt her face warm and bright with colour as she stood facing him in the dimly lit *salon*. 'Dom, you—you don't believe it, do you?'

'That you could be made jealous by her flirting with me? But of course it's nonsense!' He bent and kissed her mouth; a light gentle kiss that set her heart racing in a way that alarmed her. 'Isn't it?' he asked softly. But

Bryony did not reply; she was only thankful when he turned off that one dim light, so that he could not see her face.

It was some time since Bryony had done any diving, and at first she chafed a little at the restriction the aqua-lung harness seemed to impose on her movements. The cylinders had no weight in the water, but it wasn't quite the same sensation as swimming without restrictions of any kind, like she did when she and Tim played like a couple of energetic dolphins in the shallows.

Out here where the water was deeper there was a sense of isolation from the familiar world, where the silence was complete and vision restricted by the edge of the rubber face mask. The advantages were many, however, and one could go much deeper and see things that surface swimming did not allow sight of.

The thousands of small brightly coloured fish that swept to and fro in rainbows of movement, streaming like veils through the water, and glimpses of coral formations, and flecks of sunlight spread like nets on the surface of the sea.

Marion was close by, just off to her right, performing somersaults to Tim's encouragement, and as she turned Edward came shooting down behind her like a silent rocket from beneath the overhead bulk of the cruiser's hull, leaving a trail of silver bubbles in his wake. He slid smoothly up beside her and put a hand on her bare back, using the other to propel himself along beside her.

It wasn't possible to smile with the air-inlet clamped in his mouth, but his eyes smiled, and she responded instinctively, shrugging in response to his nod towards

Marion and Tim. They were apparently oblivious of anyone but each other, and not interested in joining them when Edward led the way deeper and further ahead, his hand still on her back.

He let go for a moment, jabbing downwards with a finger, obviously meaning they were to dive even deeper, and Bryony looked below them in the direction he indicated. The water was darker, like thick blue silk and without the same golden shimmer that glittered above their heads. There were rocks, she could see, and the lacy fans of coral among sea urchins and waving sea grass.

Edward came closer and put an arm around her shoulders, their flippered feet treading water for the moment while he pointed out their objective. Indistinct in the shifting pattern of water, its shape camouflaged by clinging barnacles and weed was a wreck; thin skeletal masts thickened by crustacea and flying pennants of weed that flowed back and forth with the tides.

Bryony nodded, her heart skipping with excitement at the prospect of exploring, and Edward's eyes gleamed approvingly as he took her hand. Downward they glided through the water, warm and soft on her skin, a lazy kicking movement with her legs sufficient to propel her downward with the help of her one free hand, until they hovered like birds above the sunken ship.

There was no clue as to how long it had been down there, but the sea soon clothed a wreck in its own disguise, making it a refuge for swarms of tiny fish who slid past them in a silvery grey ribbon and disappeared. Two masts, one of them broken off short, showed it to have been a schooner, and it lay half on its side with the rock that had holed it, thrust deep into its timbers.

It gave her a momentary shiver of horror to realise that the *Bonne Chance* with Tim and Louis aboard might so easily have ended like this, only such a short time ago. This was in all probability a Laminaire schooner, sunk before it could gain the quay. Shadows slid around the wheelhouse and the open hatchway yawned like a black mouth in the deck, and everywhere the tiny creatures who haunted such places clung in their millions to form a new outline, following closely on the old. The name was long vanished.

Boarding her was easy, they simply went in through the gaping hole in her side, but the hold was empty except for a few rotted and crustated containers that could have held almost anything originally. Bryony never really knew who started the rather energetic game of tag that followed their initial exploration of the wreck, but they chased one another through and around the old schooner for quite some time, enjoying the sensation of lightness and the silky smoothness of the water on their bodies.

Apparently Tim and Marion had found their own amusement, for they saw nothing of them near the sunken schooner, and they were quite content to have it so. Edward was momentarily out of sight, somewhere below the tilted stern of the wreck, and Bryony took advantage of his disappearance to seek out a better hiding place, somewhere he would not so easily find her. She found it in what had obviously once been the galley, a small and well concealed hiding place where he was unlikely to discover her.

There were no sounds to guide her as to his whereabouts, and she found herself holding her breath without really meaning to as she tried to detect some clue to his coming. He must surely be wondering where she had got to by now, and yet she had seen nothing of him.

After a while the galley seemed much too small and confining, and she looked around her with a fluttering sensation stirring in her breast, at the narrow doorway and the water-filled space that was little bigger than a large cupboard. Whether or not it meant giving herself up, she thought it was time she got out of that claustrophobic space before her imagination took off.

With one foot she pushed hard to give herself the impetus that would start her towards the doorway, but instead of the expected dart forward she was held back. Her foot with its big flipper broke through the rotted timbers of the galley floor and became wedged. Going through, the rubber web had bent upwards to pass through the hole, but it sprang back immediately and she was now trapped like a lobster caught in a pot.

She didn't notice any pain at all, only felt a cold rush of panic as she tried to free her foot and found herself held tightly by her ankle, held as firmly as if she was in a trap. She tugged hard, a frantic effort that dragged her ankle against the splintered edges of the hole and drew blood that tangled like thin red threads around her trapped limb.

The temptation to open her mouth and call out for Edward was barely resistible, but instead she clamped the air-inlet more firmly between her teeth and took a deep, slow breath to try and still the panic she felt. Her heart was thudding hard, and she could only think of the times Dominic had warned her and Tim never to go anywhere in a wreck alone.

She thought of Louis up there on deck, watching the sun on the water and thinking all was well with them down below, and she felt alarmingly helpless. A silver-grey streamer of small fish returned to their abandoned home, shimmering past in ribbon formation only inches from her face, and she looked around the confines of the galley with wide anxious eyes. Somewhere soon she must see the betraying tracery of bubbles that would tell her Edward was close by.

His continued absence began to tell on her nerves, and she made other abortive efforts to free herself, her imagination running riot as she pictured him similarly caught in another part of the wreck. But the more she pulled at her trapped foot the more firmly it seemed to become wedged, and she noticed that now the ankle was so swollen that it impeded any hope of release without help.

Her hands tightly rolled, she fought down a rising panic, taking slow deliberate breaths in an effort to control it, but there were so many possibilities. Edward might think she had returned to the boat and go to look for her there, or her air might run out before he found her.

She closed her eyes tightly for a second to shut out the silent water-filled little galley, and when she opened them again it was to see a drift of bubbles floating up past the tiny porthole. Once more she almost succumbed to the temptation to cry out, but hastily closed her lips round the air-inlet again when Edward's head came into view just above the edge of the round opening.

Bryony waved frantically, trying to catch his eye, and eventually he looked in, his eyes barely able to distinguish her in the dimness of the tiny galley. She used her arms, waving and signalling wildly, and, after what seemed like an eternity, he appeared in the doorway suddenly. As yet unaware of anything wrong, he ducked through and came to join her, reaching out to touch her cheek by way of congratulation for having remained hidden for so long.

Taking her hand, he meant to lead her back through the doorway, but she pulled him back, pointing downwards to her trapped foot, and she saw the change that came over his face; the colour change in his brown eyes, from sparkling laughter to dark anxiety. Crouching at her feet, he used both hands to try and free her, but the timbers, having given sufficiently to trap her, refused to budge another inch, and he could do nothing.

He came up beside her again, making signs with his hands that he needed a tool of some kind to prise the timbers apart, and she nodded. When he moved only a little way, however, she clung to his arm in sudden panic at being left again, so tightly that the mark of her fingers remained on his flesh even after he managed to free himself.

He held up one hand, the fingers spanned out, to indicate the time he anticipated it would take him to fetch the tool he needed, and she managed somehow to nod her understanding, her eyes making their own appeal. Just before he turned away he gave her a thumbs-up sign and pressed a finger first to his own lips and then to hers. A brief wave and a push and he had vanished again through the black doorway, leaving her once more with only the darting fish and the coldness of fear for company.

It seemed like hours since Edward had left her, and Bryony was close to tears, though she had not yet thought about the result of crying in the present circumstances. She supposed her ankle was going to be painful when she eventually got on dry land again, but at the moment it was simply numb, and she was grateful for that at least.

How long she had been there, she had no idea, but she was beginning to feel as if she was never going to be rescued. And then quite suddenly, as it had happened before, she thought she saw movement outside the porthole. Bubbles floated upwards and the next moment a familiar dark face, disguised in a rubber and perspex mask, looked in at her.

Louis! She hadn't expected Louis, and yet she should have done, she told herself in a delirium of relief. Waving a hand, she saw it briefly acknowledged before he disappeared as Edward had done, and she settled to wait for his reappearance with even more impatience. Once Louis knew that something had gone wrong, he would insist on coming himself. He would never entrust the task of freeing her to anyone else; Dominic would never have forgiven him if he had.

Her mind turned automatically once more to Dominic while she waited. He would be angry, she could safely say that without fear of being wrong. He would be concerned too, of course, but he would hide it as he always did in a savage anger that so often expressed the deep passions he was capable of and yet so seldom let show other than in anger.

Remembering other times, she crossed her own arms over her breast and imagined the warm, strong comfort of being in Dominic's arms. Of being kissed as he had

so nearly kissed her that day when Jenny had interrupted them; the hard, exciting touch of his mouth on
hers and the fierce possessive strength of his arms
around her. Even now she could close her eyes and feel
warmed and elated at the memory of it.

She was jolted quickly back to reality when a big
dark figure loomed in the doorway for a second before
ducking inside, and she felt a need to cry out in her
relief. She saw the searching, questioning look in his
eyes as he sought for injury other than the trapped foot
even while he was making his way in through the narrow entrance.

He had simply stripped off his shirt and put on the
diving lung, and his dark torso gleamed like polished
mahogany in the shifting uncertain light as he looked
at her through the narrow window of the mask, seeking
reassurance that she was unhurt. Bryony nodded, closing her eyes in relief and having to hold on to the air-
let in her mouth so that she did not let escape the sob
she could barely restrain, and let in water with the same
breath.

Louis crouched down beside her as Edward had
done, a heavy crowbar in his hands, and while she
stood with a hand on his shoulder he broke through
the boards next to the ones holding her foot trapped.
Muscles knotted in his arms and shoulders, he prised
at the encrusted timbers until they yielded, almost
falling backwards when it happened. A brief inspection
of her ankle brought a thumbs-up sign and a brighter,
happier look to the dark eyes behind the mask, and he
put an encouraging arm to help her start forward.

She had not realised until she swam back with Louis
just how far she and Edward had come to find the

wreck, and she was on the verge of collapse when they broke surface at last, and were helped aboard by three willing and anxious pairs of hands. Shaking the water from his black hair, Louis threaded his fingers through it, the sun already drying his slacks as well as the wet prints their feet had left on the deck.

He picked Bryony up before Edward even thought about it, and carried her to the only shaded spot there was, setting her down very carefully before bending to make a more thorough examination of her injured foot. 'Not too bad,' he decided after a second or two, 'but the sooner we get you back an' let Grand'mère fix it the better. That foot goin' to hurt plenty pretty soon, *petite*.'

'It looks pretty bad to me.' Edward obviously considered the apparently light estimation of her injuries not good enough, and he peered at the swollen ankle with a serious frown. 'You should have a doctor, Bryony.'

Feeling as she was at present, Bryony cared little who treated her, but she had to support Louis's opinion. Marie had always attended their minor ailments and injuries skilfully and successfully, and a swollen ankle was well within her capabilities.

'Marie will see to it when I get home,' she said, and Louis once more ran his hands through his hair as he stood looking down at her.

'You know you goin' to get it fierce from Monsieur Laminaire for this,' he reminded her. 'He tol' you never to go near them wrecks lessen you got somebody with you.'

'I had Ned with me, Louis; and please don't nag, my head feels as if it's going to burst, it aches so much.'

'You're not going to tell him, Louis!'

Tim was looking at him as if he could not believe him capable of such treachery, and Louis's dark eyes showed hurt for a moment. 'I ain't gon' tell him anythin', Tim, but Bryony gon' to—I know her!'

Edward, crouching beside her, looked up at Louis's tall broad figure and frowned his disapproval. It was unlikely, Bryony thought in a vague, hazy way as she gazed from one to the other through half-closed lids, that he would understand the closeness that existed between the inhabitants of Petitnue. Louis was so much more than an employee, just as Marie was, and all the other people who had lived on the island and been a part of its history for so many years.

'Louis's right, Ned.' She thought even her voice sounded unlike its usual self, husky and slightly unsteady. 'I shall tell Dominic what happened; how could I do anything else?'

'And he'll—tell you off?' He made a short angry sound that scorned her admission, and straightened up, half turning to Tim for confirmation. 'But surely you don't have to always do as you're told, like you did when you were a little girl? It doesn't make sense for a grown woman, for heaven's sake!'

Bryony's head felt as if it would burst and she was limp as a rag doll as she leaned back against hot shiny boards with her legs stretched out in front of her. Her swollen ankle was already beginning to throb painfully, just as Louis had warned it would.

'It isn't a question of doing as I'm told,' she denied fretfully, 'but we've always promised Dom we'd never go in anywhere alone if we go exploring wrecks. This is the first time I've ever done so, and with what result you can see for yourself!'

'A sheer accident!' Edward looked slightly more uneasy suddenly, as if the possible consequences of what had happened only now occurred to him, and he bent down beside her once more. 'I'm sorry this had to happen, Bryony, but you can't be blamed for it. It was just rotten luck, and just when we were enjoying ourselves too!'

She put up her hands to brush the wet hair from her neck. It was almost as dark as his now, although the copper glints were already beginning to show as it dried in the sun, and she closed her eyes to ease the glare of the bright light.

Edward could say what he liked about it being no one's fault, but nothing he said could change anything in the slightest. She knew quite well how Dominic was going to react, and she hated knowing that he was going to blame her. She didn't want him to blame her, but to hold her in his arms and comfort her, as she had imagined it while she waited alone down there in that small, dim galley for someone to come and rescue her.

She wanted Dominic's comforting presence more than anything at the moment, and she did not understand the sudden need that overwhelmed her, to weep on the broad comfort of his shoulder and feel the hard, reassuring pressure of his arms about her. Knowing that he was far more likely to remonstrate with her than offer comfort was more than she could face at the moment, and she put her hands over her face and cried.

It was neither Tim nor Edward who stroked a gentle hand over her dark copper hair and murmured comfort as she sobbed out the reaction and fear of those awful moments below, it was Louis. Reminding her of the days when she had been a little girl and in some scrape that Dominic was bound to disapprove of, the deep, sing-song accent offered hope.

'He be so glad you come back safe, he not be too angry, *petite*, you see!'

CHAPTER NINE

DOMINIC had said very little so far about her injury, but Bryony suspected it was only a matter of time. He was probably waiting until Marion and Edward had gone, which would be some time this morning, and then he would want to know how she came to be exploring a wreck on her own. Once or twice last night at dinner she had caught his eye, but it had told her nothing, not even if he thought her foolish or not.

Jules had been both teasing and sympathetic, which was just what she expected of him, and Tim had scorned her being so silly as to get herself trapped, while Jenny, inevitably, was gently sympathetic. Only Dominic had failed to react as she expected him to and it puzzled her.

She admitted without hesitation that she was going to miss Marion and Edward when they left, and yet she had not been able to agree with Edward last night when he suggested that having had a taste of the outside world she would find it hard to settle to the rather solitary peace of Petitnue again. While she bathed and dressed she pondered once more on whether or not she actually did hanker after a change.

Lately she had to admit she had suffered from a curious restlessness that she could not account for, and yet whenever she contemplated leaving Petitnue she knew it wasn't the answer. She loved the island's peace and isolation, and leaving it was not the cure for her sense of unrest, she felt sure; there must be some other solution.

She put on a sleeveless cotton dress, patterned over with small blue flowers on a darker background, and brushed her red hair until it gleamed like burnished copper, pausing for a moment to look long and thoughtfully at her reflection.

The brush still in her hand, she crossed her arms over her breast and remembered, as she had yesterday, how easy it had been to respond to the feel of Dominic's arms around her, and to the touch of that hard, persuasive mouth on hers. Marion had started the suspicion, and Edward had charged her with feeling more deeply for Dominic than she admitted, but she had declared them both to be wrong. Now, as she gazed at her own reflection and hugged her arms tightly about her, she faced for the first time the possibility of them both being right.

It was a little over an hour later, when they were all packing themselves into the jeep to drive along to the quay, that the question came to mind again. Dominic had said he was driving with them to the quay, since he was needed in the sheds, and both Tim and Bryony expected him to drive. He seldom let anyone else drive him, and particularly not Tim, who he said was downright dangerous on the road.

Tim looked surprised, but he made no demur as he took the driving seat with Marion beside him, but Edward looked definitely put out when the seat next to him in the back was taken over by Dominic. Bryony, unsure for a moment what was expected of her, hesitated by the open door and looked at him with a hint of reproach in her eyes, Tim watching curiously from his place behind the wheel.

'Room for three in the back if you squash up,' he told her, and Bryony guessed that was how it would have to be.

She started to get in, and immediately Dominic lent a hand, mindful of her injured ankle as he helped her up the rather high step, then he pulled her down on to his lap and placed an arm firmly about her waist, smiling into her frankly startled face.

'It isn't far, you'll be all right on my lap, won't you, *ma petite*?' he asked, in a voice guaranteed to bring that frown of Edward's back again.

Bryony nodded, too taken aback to say anything, and Tim was grinning broadly as he started the engine, sending them off with a jolt that sent Bryony lurching back against the broad barrier of Dominic's chest. Edward obviously took a much more biased view of the strategy and his mouth pursed in obvious dislike of being so neatly out-manoeuvred.

Such an obvious ploy was so unlike Dominic that Bryony tried in vain to understand the reason for it, although she was not at all averse to sitting on his lap. One hand rested on her waist and the other held hers where it lay on her lap, while she put an arm around his neck and clung on tightly.

With Tim at the wheel, the ride was likely to be a

rough one, and she could be thrown all over the place if she did not hold on tightly. In fact Tim might almost have been doing it deliberately, she thought, and caught a bright gleam of laughter in Dominic's eyes that suggested he shared her suspicion.

Marion half-turned in her seat, and her smile was wide and beaming, taking no account of her brother's sulky expression. 'I hate leaving here, you know.' She addressed herself to Dominic as her host, her eyes missing nothing of the way he held on to Bryony, holding her hand as well as keeping an arm around her. 'I've had a marvellous time, Dominic, and you've been marvellous to put up with us the way you have.'

'It's been a pleasure.' When he smiled his grey eyes had a warmth that Bryony knew would be irresistible to her impressionable friend. 'Bryony's loved having you here, and as for putting up with you——' He shrugged his expressive shoulders and laughed. 'You've been very considerate guests.'

'Thank you!' Marion laughed and her dark eyes were glowingly appreciative of the compliment. 'I'm only sorry that poor Bryony had to get hurt on our last day, but thank heaven it wasn't nearly as serious as it might have been.'

'And you were hardly to blame for that, were you?' Bryony, in the curve of his arm, stiffened unconsciously as she anticipated the blame she had been expecting would come her way since yesterday, but instead Dominic merely shrugged. 'Accidents happen!'

The encircling arm tightened suddenly and Bryony was thrown violently against him when Tim braked sharply at the edge of the stone quay. Momentarily off balance, she looked up to find him smiling and the grey eyes watching her enquiringly as she pushed herself upright again. There was something infinitely disturbing about the nearness of him this morning; about the aura of almost earthy virility, of bare brown arms and a slash of brown throat in the open neck of a white shirt, and she felt her pulse racing wildly as he held her.

'O.K.?' he asked, and she nodded.

When she stood to get out of the jeep, he put both hands at her waist, his fingers gripping her firmly in case she was unsure on her injured foot, and instantly Edward was out of his seat and round the other side to help her too. He handed her down the step and kept hold of her hands, looking into her face with an earnestness she found hard to face at the moment.

Dominic stepped over the side, his long legs making easy work of getting past her, then he once more placed a hand on her waist and smiled down at her. 'Don't stand too long on that ankle, *ma petite*, hmm? Say your goodbyes and then drive back in the jeep; don't attempt your usual walk through the groves, will you?'

'No, of course not, Dom.'

'Ah, you think I should take your common sense for granted, huh?' He laughed, then bent swiftly and brushed her forehead with his lips. 'I know you too well, *chérie*!' Leaving her feeling slightly light-headed and much too preoccupied to think much about her friend's departure, he shook hands with Edward and gallantly kissed Marion's hand, a gesture she accepted with a bright flush of colour and bright, excited eyes.

If only she knew what had got into him, Bryony thought hazily as, walking in line abreast, they all four went along the quay to where Edward's boat was moored, watched over by Louis. As if by mutual con-

sent Bryony and Marion walked on a little beyond the
mooring and stood at the end of the quay looking at the
bright sun on the water, and the sweep of low slung
palm trees around the point.

'Ah, well——' Marion gave an exaggerated sigh. 'It's
all over!'

'You *have* enjoyed it?'

Marion nodded unhesitatingly. 'Of course I have—
it's been super.' She grinned mischievously and glanced
at Tim engaged in rather desultory conversation with a
still disgruntled Edward. 'And Dominic doesn't have to
bother that I'm going to become the great romance in
Tim's life, you know, Bry. I know Tim better than that,
and myself as well.'

It never failed to surprise her how astute Marion
could be, and she remembered Dominic's expressed
opinion of her with a twinge of uneasiness. 'He'd rather
you were than Sarah Bryant,' she told her. 'He said so.'

'Hmm!' Clearly Marion had no difficulty in adding
the necessary qualification to that, and she smiled,
glancing over her shoulder at the loading sheds where
Dominic had disappeared. 'I hadn't realised until this
morning just how—how *French* he is.'

It was something that Bryony had always been very
aware of, and she laughed at the idea of it not being as
obvious to everyone else. 'Oh, but of course, he's
French! He's not half English like Jules and Tim are,
you know. His father as well as his mother was French.
The Laminaires might have been born in the West
Indies for the past three hundred years, but Dom's as
French as—as Paris or the Seine, or the—the Eiffel
Tower!'

'And you love him.'

Bryony caught her breath, unwilling even now to recognise the possibility of it, and she shook her head, though with little conviction she realised when she saw Marion's smile.

'You're determined, aren't you, Marion?' She laughed, but her hands were trembling as she held them close together in front of her and she carefully avoided looking directly at Marion.

'I'm right,' Marion said firmly, and touched her arm with a finger-tip. 'Don't you realise it yet, Bryony?'

'I realise that if Dom thinks it's even remotely likely he'll ship me off to Aunt Germyn in England before I have time to turn around!'

'Oh, Bry, he wouldn't!'

'He would—I know him!' And she did, she told herself, better than anyone else did, just as Jenny had once told her.

Marion obviously doubted it, but Edward and Tim were almost on them now and there was no time to say anything else, something for which Bryony was grateful as she turned to smile at Edward. He still looked slightly sulky and it was clear that he saw himself as wronged in some way, though she could not imagine how she could have behaved any differently than she had towards him without giving him quite the wrong impression.

He shook hands with Tim, then turned and took Bryony into his arms and kissed her with such fervour that she eventually struggled to free herself. Breathless and flushed, she tried not to remember that Dominic could quite easily have witnessed Edward's latest determined attempt to influence her.

'I *will* see you again, won't I, Bryony?' Marion was

watching closely, her eyes half curious, half sympathetic, perhaps feeling for her impressionable brother. But Bryony's hesitation was enough for Edward; stepping back, he let his hands fall from her arms and his head shook jerkily as if he regretted that impulsive kiss. 'I *see*!'

'Ned, I have enjoyed having you here; it's been great fun, hasn't it?'

He took a moment or two before he smiled, and then it was a small and rather rueful one as he nodded his head. 'It's been fun,' he agreed.

She gave him her hand and, after a second or two, he took it, just brushing her fingers before he let it go again. 'Goodbye, Ned.'

He was already half turned back towards the boat that bobbed against the quay, waiting for him. 'Goodbye, Bryony!'

It was, she felt, a very final-sounding goodbye.

Bryony was sitting alone in the *salon* resting her injured ankle when Dominic sought her out just after lunch. She looked up and smiled when she saw him, but blinked uncertainly when he looked so serious.

'Is something wrong?'

She couldn't imagine what could be wrong, but something was on his mind, that much was clear. He sat with his hands clasped together and his elbows resting on his knees, in the chair next to hers, and she could see the fine lines that ran from the corners of his eyes to the thick dark hair at the side of his head.

It was a good face, she decided, watching the shadows that deepened and darkened the outline of high cheek bones and a strong jaw. His mouth was wide, but it had a strength that could show in the firm straight line of anger, and a gentleness that could kiss away a child's tears when she wanted so desperately to stay home instead of being sent back to school. It was a face she loved, she realised, and hastily shifted her gaze when he looked up suddenly and caught her eyes on him.

'I've had a letter from your great-aunt,' he said, and for a moment Bryony stared at him uncomprehendingly.

Then slowly she shook her head, her heart hammering hard in her breast suddenly as she prepared to fight tooth and nail not to be sent away again. 'I—I don't see——' she began, but Dominic cut her short.

'You didn't answer her when she wrote to you, did you, *ma petite*?'

She hadn't written to Aunt Germyn, she remembered, because it had completely gone out of her mind. In any case, she had nothing to say to someone who wanted to disrupt her life as it was, and she could think of no polite way of telling the old lady so.

'I forgot—I did really,' she added hastily when she looked up and saw his smile of disbelief. 'Anyway, Dom, what could I say to her? All those things—those silly things she said in her letter; what could I say to them?'

He did not attempt to answer her, but instead produced a page from his pocket bearing the familiar thin scrawl in black ink and handed it to her. She took it only reluctantly, and found its contents discomfitingly similar to those of her own letter.

She considered it wise to send Bryony to England for a time, so that she could see something of her mother's family, and also, as the old lady put it, give some thought to her present situation, which was to say the least unconventional. She felt sure, Miss Germyn continued, that he, as a man of the world, would understand her point of view and she was sure he was gentleman enough to realise her fears.

'Shall I write to her?' she ventured, handing back the paper as if she hated the touch of it. 'I could write this afternoon, Dom, and tell her I'm staying here.' He hadn't immediately lent his support to the idea, and that worried her so that she looked across at him anxiously. 'Dom?'

It was always difficult to know what was going on in his mind and he was careful in this instance to keep the dark lashes lowered sufficiently to hide the look in his eyes. He held the folded page and folded and refolded it into a tiny square before he said anything.

'I've been wondering, Bryony, whether you *should* go—on a visit, of course. You are English, after all, and you haven't set foot in England since you were ten years old.'

Bryony's heart was pounding so hard her head ached with it, and she was staring at him in frank dismay. Clasping her hands tightly, she looked down at them rather than at him after a moment because it hurt to realise that she loved him so much and he was so anxious to send her away.

'You—you think I should go?' She scarcely believed it; she didn't want to believe it, but those carefully evasive eyes were hardly reassuring.

'You've seen very little of the rest of the world since you came here, *ma chère*.' His hands moved in a vaguely helpless way that was so unlike him that she felt her heart turn cold and heavy in her breast. 'Perhaps you should see other places, other people; make comparisons. Since you left school you've known so few people that you can't really know——' Again that unfamiliar air of helplessness touched sensitive nerves, and she caught her breath hastily.

'I know how I feel, it's only your feelings I can't understand, but if that's what you want me to do—go away, somewhere, to England or anywhere——' Her voice was small and, she realised with dismay, alarmingly unsteady. 'It's your home after all, Dom, and I'm only here on sufferance since Papa died; I do realise that!'

'Bryony!'

She couldn't stand any more, she thought wildly, she had to go where she couldn't see him. Where she could sit and think without the sight of him to drive home just how much she wanted to stay with him, and she got to her feet, clumsy because her ankle reminded her rather sharply that it was far from healed.

In the doorway she half turned, but she didn't look at him, only allowed him to see the tremulous lower lip that quivered threateningly, and the defiant toss of her copper-red head as she went out. 'I've got a lot of thinking to do,' she told him huskily. 'Please excuse me!'

No matter how long she thought about it, it didn't hurt any less, knowing how ready Dominic was to send her to her great-aunt, and she wished she could cry, it would have relieved her feelings to some extent. Instead she sat dry-eyed and abjectly miserable, staring out at the deep blue sea under its golden net, where a schooner dipped with the trades and skimmed across the surface in a trail of spindrift, like scattered snow.

She didn't have to go back to England, she told herself, she could stay in the islands and perhaps get a job. Marion would know someone who could give her work, and even Dominic admitted that she was good with figures. It wouldn't be the same as here on Petitnue, of course, nowhere could, but at least she would be a little nearer to Dominic than if she was on the other side of the world.

She started when she heard someone coming across the sand behind her, and half-turned expecting it to be Tim, for this was their favourite beach. 'Bryony.'

She got to her feet, ready to run she realised with a start, when she recognised Dominic's deep and unmistakable voice, and when she turned to face him, her eyes were wide, almost desperate, in their appeal. She felt a sense of helplessness suddenly and the tears that had refused to comfort her earlier now streamed down her face as she looked at him.

'Ah, *ma petite*!'

He took her in his arms as he had so often done when she was in need of comfort, and held her close with his face resting on the silky red softness of her hair. But there was more than just comfort in his arms this time, she realised, and closed her eyes as she let the warmth of his nearness flow over her, recalling how he had held her with the same possessive fierceness once before. When Jenny had made her inopportune entrance into the office one day.

'Don't cry, *chérie*—ssh, *mon amie, s'il te plaît*!'

Bryony lifted her face to look at him, her eyes bright but still misty with tears and her mouth tremblingly unsteady as she gazed at him with parted lips. 'You—

you said you wanted me to go away.'

He made a wry face at the accusation, and his mouth hinted at a smile. 'I mused aloud, *ma petite*; you have heard me do so before. I was considering the wisdom of letting you see something more of the world than Petitnue—and me!'

He was looking at her with such intensity that she could feel her body responding to the force that made him hold her so tightly, and her own breast echoed the hard strong beat of his heart. 'Oh, Dom, I——'

'Did you really believe that I wanted to send you away?'

'I don't know!' She remembered the times she had tried to read what was going on behind those unfathomable grey eyes, and failed. 'I've *never* known what you want, how you feel! When I was at school and you used to send me back after I'd been home, I hated it, and you were always so—so gentle and sweet to me, but you still made me go back!'

'Because I had to, *chérie*, you must have known that.'

'And now?'

The grey eyes warmed and smiled and she felt her heart expand like a flower in the sun when he bent and kissed her lightly on her mouth. 'Now you go only if you want to, *petite*! I can't pretend I want you to, I can't even think about it any more.'

'Oh, Dom!'

She buried her head against him until a hand in her hair pulled her head back and the grey eyes searched her face, a fierce, intense scrutiny that sent shivering thrills all through her body until she literally trembled with emotions she scarcely recognised.

Then his face filled her vision for a moment; grey

eyes, dark and unfathomable, and a mouth that promised the kisses she hungered for; the dark craggy features that she loved more than life itself. His arms tightened and drew her so close she could feel every muscle that strained her to him, and the warm smoothness of tanned skin tempted her to open his shirt with her finger-tips and stroke lightly while she kept her eyes only as high as his firm strong jaw.

Then his mouth touched hers lightly and she reached up to draw down his dark head closer still, stretching up to press as close as she could, until he buried his mouth in hers and she seemed to have stopped breathing. Then his voice was close to her ear and his lips pressed to the warm soft skin of her neck as she half-opened her eyes to look up at the incredible blueness of the sky between feathery palm leaves.

'I wish I could teach you French, right at this moment, *mon amie*!'

Her whisper of laughter stirred the hair at the nape of his neck and he lifted his head to look at her, a large hand still cradling the back of her head, long fingers teasing the thick, silky red hair. The grey eyes swept slowly over her face and she smiled at him with her parted lips soft and inviting, hungry for his kisses.

'If you spoke my language I could say so much better how much I love you!' He kissed the side of her neck, nuzzling her ear while he spoke. 'Only in French can I do you justice, *ma belle petite amie*!'

He whispered to her in his own tongue, his mouth emphasising each softly spoken word with a kiss, and Bryony asked no more than to be allowed to stay there for ever as they were. His arms holding her close and his voice murmuring those whispered words in her ear.

When she had breath enough, she looked up into his face and smiled, a small and very satisfied smile that made him bend his head and kiss her once more. 'Shall I write to Aunt Germyn or will you?' she asked, and Dominic considered for a moment, so that she immediately took it upon herself. 'I'd like to,' she told him with a hint of mischief. 'I can't wait to tell her that I'm staying here with you after all.'

A gleam of laughter lit Dominic's grey eyes and he kissed her mouth slowly. 'Better tell her you're going to marry me, *ma chérie*, it will sound better!'

'I'd stay anyway!' She lifted her face to him and her heart beat so hard she could not control the shivery sound of her voice. 'I love you, Dom, I think I always have.'

Dominic was shaking his head and the smile in his grey eyes warmed her even more than the bright Caribbean sun. 'This is not like always, *mon amour*,' he said softly. 'You will see!'

Harlequin
Announces the
COLLECTION
EDITIONS
OF 1978

Harlequin's Collection 12

ANDREA BLAKE

Night of the Hurrica...

Harlequin's Collection 106   1.25

ANNE WEALE

If This Is Love

stories of special
beauty and significance

25 Beautiful stories of particular merit

In 1976 we introduced the first 100 Harlequin Collections — a selection of titles chosen from our best sellers of the past 20 years. This series, a trip down memory lane, proved how great romantic fiction can be timeless and appealing from generation to generation. Perhaps because the theme of love and romance is eternal, and, when placed in the hands of talented, creative, authors whose true gift lies in their ability to write from the heart, the stories reach a special level of brilliance that the passage of time cannot dim. Like a treasured heirloom, an antique of superb craftsmanship, a beautiful gift from someone loved, — these stories too, have a special significance that transcends the ordinary.

Here's your 1978 Harlequin Collection Editions . . .

More great Harlequin 1978 Collection Editions . . .

122 Moon Over Africa
Pamela Kent
(#983)

123 Island In The Dawn
Averil Ives
(#984)

124 Lady In Harley Street
Anne Vinton
(#985)

125 Play The Tune Softly
Amanda Doyle
(#1116)

126 Will You Surrender?
Joyce Dingwell
(#1179)

Original Harlequin Romance numbers in brackets

Send for your copy today!

The Harlequin Romance Catalog FREE!

Here's your chance to catch up on all the wonderful Harlequin Romance novels you may have missed because the books are no longer available at your favorite booksellers.

Complete the coupon and mail it to us. By return mail, we'll send you a copy of the latest Harlequin catalog. Then you'll be able to order the books you want directly from us.

Clip and mail coupon today.